Return to
BITTER CREEK

Return to BITTER CREEK

A NOVEL BY
Doris Buchanan Smith

VIKING KESTREL

To Jingle
who knows all my ranges
from bitter to sweet

VIKING KESTREL

Viking Penguin Inc., 40 West 23rd Street, New York, New York 10010, U.S.A.
Penguin Books Ltd, 27 Wrights Lane, London W8 5TZ (Publishing & Editorial) and
Harmondsworth, Middlesex, England (Distribution & Warehouse)
Penguin Books Australia Ltd, Ringwood, Victoria, Australia
Penguin Books Canada Limited, 2801 John Street, Markham, Ontario, Canada L3R 1B4
Penguin Books (N.Z.) Ltd, 182-190 Wairau Road, Auckland 10, New Zealand

Copyright © Doris Buchanan Smith, 1986
All rights reserved
First published in 1986 by Viking Penguin Inc.
Published simultaneously in Canada
Printed in USA
by The Book Press, Brattleboro, Vermont
Set in Garamond
3 4 5 90 89 88

Library of Congress Cataloging in Publication Data
Smith, Doris Buchanan.   Return to Bitter Creek.
Summary: An illegitimate child in the South learns
the meaning of love and family life.
[1. Family life—Fiction. 2. Southern States—Fiction] I. Title.
PZ7.S64474Re 1986   [Fic]   85-40838   ISBN 0-670-80783-4

Contents

Trillium 3

Bitter Creek 11

The Barn 23

Sunday Dinner 33

Ridgewire 38

Choices 47

Summer Roots 57

Flat Rock Days 64

The Wildflower Connection 72

Fences 82

Polly 95

The Cabin 110

No Forevers 119

Moving 125

The Ice Palace 135

Dancing 145

Equal Partners 158

Trillium 167

Return to
BITTER CREEK

Trillium

THE CLOSER THEY CAME TO BITTER CREEK THE MORE
Lacey knew what the least of their problems would be.
Explaining that David's name was pronounced Dah-veed
would be the easy part. The hard part had been under
discussion all the way from the Colorado Rockies to the
Appalachians of North Carolina.

"I still say we should go to your parents first thing,"
David said.

Lacey's mother, Campbell, made the same response she'd
made for all these miles. "No."

Leaning back with her eyes closed, Lacey let the vibra-
tions of the moving truck hum through her body and the

words of the disagreement pass over it. She sat between them in the cab of the pickup, all their belongings jouncing along in the truck bed behind. David was a blacksmith, and he thought he could forge a bond in the relationship between Lacey's mother and grandparents as easily as he melded metal on the anvil.

"We'll melt them," he kept saying. But melting required heat, Lacey knew, and Campbell was acting exceedingly cool. Without moving or opening her eyes, Lacey smiled as he said it again. David was an expert melter. He'd melted her and Campbell three years ago, and they hadn't solidified since.

"Is that Bitter Creek?" David asked. As the truck slowed, Lacey twisted around to watch. The utility trailer swayed as David turned onto a gravel road and crossed a rickety plank bridge. In the trailer was David's blacksmithing equipment. The back of the truck was filled with boxes of clothing, cookware, dishes, Campbell's leatherwork, and the microwave oven. Folded plumply in between was David's Indian-style mattress which, with a flip and a flop, could be turned into a sofa.

For a moment it seemed to Lacey that the whole of Colorado was in that truck bed. Except for the old rocker, her entire life was here in the truck. The rocker was Campbell's life, the only thing besides Lacey that her mother had dragged across the country when she'd fled west ten years ago when Lacey was two. She settled back into the seat as the truck and trailer came to a halt. She was, she thought, both cool and warm, both anxious and curious to meet her grandparents, afraid but longing, too.

David bounded out of the truck and Lacey slid out behind him and raced him to the creek.

"There's nothing bitter about this water," he said, sipping from cupped hands. His dark hair fell across his forehead. Lacey brushed back her own. She took in a deep breath of the crisp mountain air and let her eyes be dazzled by the meteor showers of dogwood in the otherwise still-brown woods. Redipping his hands, David offered his "cup" to Lacey. She laughed and slurped. They both knew that the "bitter" of Bitter Creek had nothing to do with the water. The creek was originally named Bittner Creek, a family name, her and Campbell's name. When the Appalachian tongue got wound around a word, Campbell said, it often added something or left off something. In this case it was the *n* in Bittner.

"Don't you two ever walk anywhere?" Campbell asked, coming up and squatting beside them. She had pulled a multicolored knit cap over her head and it made her hair spring out at odd angles to the ears. Campbell's hair was dark, too. Lacey liked it that they all looked a bit alike, square and sturdy and, as David called their dark complexions, swarthy.

David held out a hand-cup of water to Campbell, then anointed her forehead with his damp hands. "I declare you Her Royal Highness, Campbell Bittner, Queen of Bitter Creek," he said. As he repeated the gesture on Lacey, a trickle eased down to the tip of her nose. She stuck out her tongue to catch it as it dropped. "And you," he said, "are just a drip!" He hooked an arm over each of their shoulders and kissed Campbell's cheek. "I love your Bitter Creek."

"For better or worse," Campbell said. Lacey watched her stare off into space, then saw her eyes focus on something. "Look! the trillium are in bloom."

Lacey and David followed Campbell's gaze. In the spring woods of the rising ridge across the creek were dozens, hundreds, thousands of nodding flowers.

"*Trillium cernuum*," Campbell said. "Nodding trillium."

"How do you know that?" Lacey asked. "The Latin name?"

"Oh, la, I grew up with it," Campbell said. "My mama knows the name of everything."

Instead of joy in *Trillium cernuum*, the loss of Colorado hit Lacey so fast and hard she tasted salt. Columbine, she knew. But what were all those other things she'd grown up with and never learned the names of? There was a distinct empty space, too, where a grandmother should have been all these years, a grandmother who knew the name of everything.

When they were back at the truck, David asked, "Where's the town of Bitter Creek?"

"We'll come to it soon enough," Campbell said. "Just keep going the way you were going to get to the Craft School." The Mountain Craft School was the reason they were here, not from any wish of Campbell's to return to her childhood home. The Craft School had wanted a blacksmith. David had applied and been hired, all the way from Clio, Colorado, to Bitter Creek, North Carolina.

6

The road was narrow and winding. Around one curve, some buildings came quickly into view. "Is that them?" David asked, pressing his foot to the brake as they whizzed past.

"Don't you dare stop," Campbell said.

Lacey looked back quickly at the red and blue buildings, one on each side of the road. "Is that them?" she asked. Her grandparents' store? Her Uncle Kenny's garage? Campbell didn't answer and David didn't stop.

At the Mountain Craft School, they met a hearty hand-shaker who identified herself as Ms. Lamb, Patricia Lamb. "Bittner! I had no idea that David was bringing home-folks," she said. "Are you Bitter Creek Bittners?"

"We are," Campbell said. "Or used to be. And will be again now we're here."

At least Ms. Lamb said David's name right, Lacey noted.

"Who are your people?" Ms. Lamb asked as they walked down a woodsy path toward the blacksmith shop. Lacey saw more trillium.

"The Bittners of the Gas and Gro.," Campbell said. The two women laughed at Campbell's abbreviation.

"You're a native all right," said Patricia Lamb.

"That's what's painted on the window," Campbell explained to David and Lacey, "so we always called it the Gas and Gro."

"So, you're Kenny's sister," Ms. Lamb said. She had opened the door of an ancient-looking wood and stone building and they walked through, David touching anvils, hammers, clamps, tongs. Lacey looked at Ms. Lamb, trying to read her face. What had the woman heard about Ann Campbell Bittner, who had run away with a rocking chair and a child ten years ago? "Kenny, Marlene, and the girls often come to the dances on Saturday nights."

Campbell nodded. "They still have the dances, then."

"Forever and ever, I hope," said Ms. Lamb.

"For sight unseen I made out very well," David said, pausing in his inspection. "I hope you soon decide the same about me."

"I'm sure we will," said Ms. Lamb. "We were very impressed with your qualifications."

The old Ford place, which they were going to rent, was down a long driveway, along the edge of woods and an old field. "I wish I could offer you housing on campus," Ms. Lamb had said, repeating what had already been said in a letter. "But under the circumstances—" The only thing that bothered Lacey about the circumstances was the people who kept calling it the circumstances. She shrugged it off as she and Campbell handed boxes down from the truck. At least Ms. Lamb had pronounced David's name correctly: Dah-veed Hah-beeb. Most people, even when they heard David say it himself, insisted on using the more familiar Day-vid. And they made all kinds of wrong stabs at Habib.

"Praise be, a woodpile," David said as he spotted the stack on the small front porch.

"I hope that means a fireplace and not a woodstove," Campbell said.

David laughed and handed Lacey the key to unlock the door. "We've cooked on a lot less," he said.

And lived in a lot less, Lacey thought as she opened the door. When they'd met David, they were living in a barn and so was he. She'd kind of liked living in the barn amid the smell of hay and horses, but a house was nice. The woodpile was for a fireplace that was in the kitchen, along with a modern gas range and an electric refrigerator.

"And look," David said, teasing. "Real running water. We won't have to haul it from the spring. Your microwave will not be alone."

They'd laughed gleefully over the microwave, which was such an unlikely object for them to have. Campbell had won it in a drawing at a grocery store. David had assumed they'd sell it, but Campbell said, "No. It's the only thing I ever won in my life."

David set the microwave on the kitchen counter and returned to the truck for the mattress. He shoved the dinette set aside with his hip and let the mattress flop to the floor in front of the fireplace. "I love you," he said to Campbell, and pulled her down onto the mattress for a hug. "You, too, Old Lace," he said, looking up at Lacey.

"I know," she said, and she stepped to look out the window. There were comets of dogwood all through the woods here, too, and something orange that Campbell had said was flame azalea. When she breathed in, the kitchen smelled musty, as though no one had lived here for a while. When she breathed out, she leaned close and fogged the glass. Pressing a fingertip against the smooth, cool pane, she wrote in the vapor, US.

Bitter Creek

WHILE THE TASTE OF SYRUP AND SAUSAGE WAS STILL on Lacey's tongue, David said, "Well."

"Well what?" Campbell asked, flopping back down onto the mattress in front of the freshly stoked fire. Lacey scraped leftover pancakes into the garbage and slid the sticky breakfast plates into the sudsy water.

"Avoiding it won't make it any easier," David said, walking over and standing beside the mattress. He and Campbell had slept there, before the fire, while Lacey had been banished to one of the two bedrooms. Even without the warmth of the togetherness and the fire, she'd slept well on the unfamiliar bed with her familiar brightly striped sheets.

Campbell grabbed David's ankles and toppled him onto the mattress and began tickling and kissing him. He enfolded her into a bear hug and tried to hoist her to her feet. She went limp.

"Come on, Lacey, help me," David said.

"I'm not getting into the middle of that," she said, continuing with the dishes. She dribbled liquid soap onto the inside of one thumb and curled her index finger to the base of the thumb and back up to the tip. She blew gently but firmly into this self-made bubble-wand and a bubble the size of a tennis ball formed and separated from her hand. The entire world of the kitchen floated in miniature rainbow curves and she peered at it to find herself.

"I'll get you," David said from behind Lacey. She could see him in the bubble but couldn't tell what he was doing. She turned and saw him rolling Campbell up inside the mattress. Head and feet sticking out of the ends of the roll, Campbell giggled as David tugged the bedroll through the doorway, calling on Lacey again to help. With the assurance of Campbell's laughter, Lacey dried her hands and shoved as David pulled.

"No, no, no!" Campbell cried when David tugged the bundle upright at the front door. But she was still laughing.

"Yes, yes, yes!" David said, punctuating each yes with a kiss as he let the mattress fall away.

As David edged Campbell out the door, Lacey grabbed her knitted jacket, a multicolored match to Campbell's hat. She liked all colors and didn't know how anyone could choose a favorite. Well, orange, maybe, she thought as a flame azalea caught her eye.

"I thought this was the South," she said as she climbed into the pickup ahead of Campbell. There was a Colorado bite to the April air.

"It's the mountain south," Campbell said, pulling on the matching cap and jacket she'd left in the truck. "We'll have frost again yet."

With fear and excitement, Lacey stared at the road as they drove the two miles to Bitter Creek. Brown tangles of tree trunks and limbs seemed to fall back and away, as though the truck were a boat and the trees were the wake. From the right, a glint of silver flashed where the creek rimmed the road. Then, around one last curve, the two red and blue buildings popped into sight. As David drove past the gas pumps and up to the boardwalk that was like a sidewalk in front of the store, Lacey read the lettering on the glass.

BITTNER'S GAS AND GRO.
EVA AND THOMAS BITTNER, PROPS.

David got out but when Campbell didn't move, Lacey didn't scramble after him as she usually did. David came around and opened the passenger door.

"Come on," he said. "It will be fine. You'll see."

Campbell slid down then, and Lacey followed as though attached to her mother by a tether. David opened the door and stood back for Campbell and Lacey to precede him.

The store was dim, with gray-painted concrete floors—

13

not all tile and fluorescent lights like the supermarkets Lacey was used to. There was only one counter, right at the front of the store. A woman in a red pants suit, who looked as much like Campbell as Lacey did, looked up from where she was restocking a shelf with cigarettes.

"Yes?" the woman said, and in midword Lacey saw the sign of recognition come into the woman's eyes. "Ann?" Question marks were on cheeks, eyes, and brow as well as tongue. Then a shriek. "Ann?!"

"Yes, Mama," Campbell said, and she and her mother met in a hug at the end of the counter.

"Ann, Ann."

"Mama."

"Ann. Lacey? Tom, come quick. It's Ann come home." The women hugged and hugged and then beckoned to Lacey, who joined the hug. Lacey glanced back at David, wanting him inside the hug, too, but he shook his head and stayed back.

"Oh, Lacey, Lacey, child. How I've missed you. How I've thought of you. How I've wanted you back home in Bitter Creek."

A man in jeans and a red-checkered shirt came toward them. "Oh, my, oh," was all he managed to say as he joined the hugging. Then Campbell and Lacey were passed back and forth. Grandmother's hugs were fierce, but Grandfather's were soft as the shirt he wore. Finally Grandmother pushed Lacey back at arm's length.

"Lacey, Lacey, let me look at you."

Grandfather took hold of her arm and said, "More like

rope than lace. Good and sturdy. I like that. Sturdy like Bittners are supposed to be."

The greetings ebbed and Grandmother looked up, inquiringly, as though David were a customer who had just walked in. Campbell extended an arm toward David. "Mama, Papa, this is David."

"Dah-veed? What sort of name is that?" Grandfather asked. "Where are you from, with a name like that?"

David grinned and stepped forward with his hand outstretched. "It's my name, Mr. Bittner, sir. And I'm from Colorado, if it makes any difference where a person is from."

"Sometimes it does," Grandfather said. "And I know they don't call people Dah-veed in Colorado."

"Well, that's what they called me," David said.

"David is the new blacksmith at the Craft School," Campbell said. "Perhaps you saw it in the paper." Ms. Lamb had given David a copy of the local paper with the announcement of his appointment.

"Yes, we did," Grandfather and Grandmother said in chorus. "And your other name is strange, too," Grandfather added.

"Well. We had no idea, of course—" Grandmother said. There was more nodding and arm-waving along with a few more awkwardly spaced "wells."

"So. You've finally come home," Grandmother said. "We'll shove right over and make room." She looked pointedly at David. "You'll be staying at the school, I suppose, won't you?"

Even Lacey knew the remark was more a hope than a guess. She chose a spot on the cigarette rack and stared at it.

"No, we've rented a little house a couple of miles from here," David said.

"The old Ford place," Campbell said.

"You could have let us know you'd gotten married," Grandmother said. Lacey began reading brand names and playing the alphabet game. *A* and *B* from Marlboro, *C* from Camels, *D* from Players Select Brand. She was searching for a *J* by the time Grandmother broke the silence.

"You mean you're not?" When there was still no answer, she asked, "What sort of people does that school hire?"

"I think this was the same line we were on when I left here ten years ago," Campbell said.

Grandfather took hold of Grandmother's arm and they moved back one step, leaving Lacey standing like the center dot on the five-side of a domino. "The child will, of course, stay with us," Grandfather said.

"No," Lacey said more loudly than she intended and she moved in between David and Campbell, turning them into threes and twos. The fear ringing in the echo of her voice surprised her. She was twelve years old. They wouldn't try to take her as Campbell said they had tried when she was two. They were her grandparents. They loved her, didn't they? She wanted to love them. Still, she was sorry Campbell had told them where they lived.

"How's Kenny?" Campbell said, pushing words into the space. Lacey slid her hand into her mother's. Campbell had never said much about the family but had talked, occasionally, about the fun she used to have with her brother. But in all the years away, they had not heard from him once.

"Fine. They're all fine. They'll sure be surprised to see you. The girls are so big. Teresa started school this year. Tina's in fourth. And Tam, well, she'll be going to junior high next year. Seventh grade."

"Me, too," Lacey said. "Where's the school? When can I meet my cousins? I'm glad there's one my age." She, too, threw words into the space, to cover her moment of fear, to match the chatter. "I'm meeting some Bittners at last."

"The school's in Savory," Grandmother said, and Lacey did not miss the critical look at Campbell which said, See there, you have deprived this child of her family.

"Savory!" Lacey said. "Savory and Bitter Creek. What a combination."

"Kenny's home now," Grandfather said. "At the garage. Marlene's at work and the girls are at school. You walk on across. We have to stay with the store."

David, Campbell, and Lacey crossed the narrow roadway. There was a board sidewalk in front of Kenny's, too, but it had a gap in it so cars could enter the garage. These two buildings were the entire town of Bitter Creek. These walkways, Lacey thought, gave it more the look of a western town than an eastern, mountain one. The smell of gas and oil stung Lacey's nostrils as they wandered into the tool-strewn work space. No one was in sight, but some clanking sounds came from under a car. David said

17

nothing, waiting as before for Campbell to take the lead.

"Kenny? Is that you under there?"

There was the scraping sound of wheels and a man in red coveralls emerged on his back on a flatbed cart. The man blinked. Did everyone around here wear red, Lacey wondered? The man sat up, stood up, then blinked again. "Ann? Ann? Oh, my Annnnn!" He reached for Campbell, stopped, looked at his greasy hands, swiped them on a rag, then grabbed her. "Oh, hell, I'll pay the cleaning bill," he said. By the time he released her he was weeping, wiping his arm across his eyes, smearing grease, sniffing and saying, "Shit."

He turned to a sink and scooped up a glop of cleaner and began to wash his hands.

"Goop," said Lacey. It was the same stuff David used to clean his hands, and was the first familiar thing she'd seen.

"Is that Lacey?" Kenny asked.

Lacey wondered who else he thought she might be.

"We'll go to the school and pick up the girls right now. This is a holiday. A real holiday."

"No, no, there'll be time for that," Campbell said.

"I can't get Marlene. She's an O.R. nurse. Did you know that? She got her nursing degree and she works over at Mountain Home Hospital. The doctors wouldn't appreciate it much if I went charging over there and hauled her ass out of the operating room." He scrubbed and scrubbed his hands, which still didn't come clean in the final rinse. "We didn't hear from you! We didn't know how you were," he said, ripping loose a length of paper toweling to dry his hands. "We didn't know *where* you were."

"Didn't know where we were?" Campbell said. "Mama knew where we were almost all the time."

"She knew?" Kenny said.

"Didn't she tell you whenever she heard from us?"

"Yes, but she never said where you were. Always acted like she didn't know where you were calling from." While shaking his head in disbelief, he noticed David. He turned the shake into a nod as Campbell introduced them. "Dahveed, Dah-veed," Kenny repeated, as though to imprint the pronunciation onto his brain. "Excuse the hands."

"Next time you shake with me mine will be black as well," David said. "I'm a blacksmith by trade."

"Oh?" Kenny's face lit up and he shook harder.

"I'm the new blacksmith over at the Craft School," he said.

"Oh?" Kenny said again. "David Habib. I saw that in the paper." Kenny said "Hay-bib."

"Ha-beeb," David said.

"Ha-beeb, Ha-beeb," Kenny said, laughing as he imprinted this pronunciation, too. "David Habib. Nice ring to it. You all living over at the school?"

"We've rented the old Ford place," Campbell said.

Kenny nodded. "Come to dinner. Marlene will want you to come to dinner. Hell, *I* want you to come to dinner. Mama and Papa will come over. They eat with us a lot."

"Kenny-y-y," Campbell said.

"Now don't give me any of this Kenny-y-y stuff," Kenny said.

"There will be time for all that," Campbell said. "I'm glad to see you, really, but I have to get back into these family things slowly. You know?"

"No, I don't know." He shrugged and sounded belligerent.

"I didn't exactly leave here with love at my back," Campbell said. "I've been really hurt by all this, Kenny."

"You've been hurt? What about us? You just taking off like that. Taking the baby."

"She was *my* baby, Kenny. Was I supposed to leave her?"

"Hey," David said, holding a flat-palmed hand up to each of them. "Are you glad to see her?" he asked Kenny.

"Hell, yes, I'm glad to see her. She's my sister."

"Are you glad to see him?" David asked Campbell.

"Yes," she said softly.

"Good. Hug now and talk later." Kenny and Campbell responded to David's direction and stepped together into another hug.

"Sunday, then?" Kenny asked. "Big Sunday dinner? Out on the boardwalk, if it's warm? Like we used to?"

Campbell nodded.

"And you, Lacey," Kenny put his broad hand to Lacey's back. "You stay with me and we'll go get the girls from school. Tam, at least."

"Damn it, no, Kenny," Campbell said.

Lacey blinked at her mother's outburst and Kenny removed his hand as though Lacey's back was on fire.

20

"Sunday," Campbell said, and the three of them walked back across the street. Campbell poked her head back into the store without letting her body follow. "We're going for now, Mama. We'll have dinner at Kenny's on Sunday, okay?"

"Well, what about Lacey?" Lacey heard her grandmother ask.

"What about Lacey?" Campbell asked back.

"Why don't you let her stay here?"

David touched Campbell's arm and Campbell said, "We have a lot to do and we need her help." Lacey caught hold of David's hand, relieved at Campbell's calm reply, although it was not the truth. The few things they'd brought from Colorado had been unpacked and put away yesterday.

"You mean you're working that child?" Grandmother said, her voice drifting out the door.

Campbell huffed up half a laugh. "You say that like I didn't make change at this store from the time I was eight and pump gas from the time I was ten. And you thought it was cute as pumpkin pie! Lacey's twelve years old, Mama. She can even do a little blacksmithing."

In the car on the way back to the house, Campbell carried on a monologue. "Did you hear them? Mama, Papa, Kenny, all right ready to take us over, even now? Mama would say live and let live and mean it, for everyone but me and Lacey. And Kenny, acting like he missed me so much and he never did get in touch in all these years."

"He said he didn't know where we were," Lacey said. She'd been as shocked as Campbell and Kenny that

Grandmother had never given Kenny an address.

"They don't love us," Campbell said. "They just want us as possessions."

David slid an arm around Campbell and maneuvered the curves with one hand on the steering wheel. "Come on, sweetheart. Don't make the mistake of thinking love is pure and perfect."

This remark surprised Lacey. Wasn't love the one perfect thing?

"They ran us off," Campbell said.

"That was ten years ago," said David.

Campbell held herself stiff and didn't relax against David's arm. "Hmmph," she said. "Ten years makes no difference in Bitter Creek."

The Barn

THE NEXT DAY, SATURDAY, DAVID WAS ALREADY OUT looking for a barn. Even though he could do his own work at the Craft School, he was accustomed to having his own shop. They spent the morning crisscrossing the countryside, up paved roads and down gravel ones. It was a slow, meandering trip with them discovering and Campbell rediscovering ridges, coves, and stony brooks. At one point, Campbell directed David toward Logan, a town beyond Savory and over the mountains. At the top of the mountain, the road had been blasted and sheer rock walls towered above the road.

"Stop here," Campbell said. They followed her out of

the truck and, chins tilted, looked up the precipice.

"It looks like a fortress," David said.

"A castle," said Lacey. The surface of the walls were even damp, as she imagined castle walls might be.

"A palace," Campbell said, calling their attention to that dampness. Water seeped in some places, like the condensation on a glass, and streamed down in others. "Springs," Campbell said. "In the winter when it freezes, it's a spectacle. Ablaze with ice. I call it the Ice Palace."

"Ablaze with ice. How do you like that description, Lace?" David said, teasing. Still, Lacey imagined the Ice Palace and goose pimples rose on her arms under her jacket.

For the sentiment of it, they wound up back on the dirt and gravel road they'd turned onto two days ago. The water tasted better here than anywhere else. There were more pink trillium than before and Campbell explained that the color of the blossom deepened as the flower aged. As they wandered, they noticed a barn just uphill before the mountain rose steeply behind it. The road and the plank bridge seemed to be here only for the barn. When they explored, they saw it was unused. David inquired about the owner and before long, with incredible David-luck, they had rented a barn.

They ate the sandwiches they'd brought inside the barn amid the dust of past harvests. Campbell walked around touching the weathered wood, picking up an old piece of harness, pushing a toe in the dirt floor.

"This could be Papa's barn. I think all these old barns are alike."

"Does Grandfather have a barn?" Lacey asked.

"Of course. Everybody has a barn, Lacey," Campbell said.

"Where is it?"

"Behind the house."

"Right there in town?" Though she hadn't seen the house, Lacey knew from Campbell that the back of her grandparents' house adjoined the back of the store.

"Town?" Campbell laughed. "In Bitter Creek and Savory, Lacey, the farms are in town, right up to the stores, right up to the road. Now, in Mountain Home and Logan, you have regular sorts of neighborhoods, but even there, they have farms right up to the edge of town."

"Is Mountain Home the name of a town?" Lacey asked.

"Mountain Home is the metropolis hereabout," Campbell said. "It's at the other end of the valley from Savory, out past the Craft School. Biggest place around unless you go over the mountain to Logan."

Lacey nodded, feeling she was getting her bearings a bit, even though she had not yet been either to Logan or Mountain Home.

"You know what this barn means, don't you?" Campbell asked David.

"Well, I know what it means to me," he said, "but I can tell by your tone of voice that you're thinking something else entirely."

"It means we'll have to come past Mama's every time we go and come."

"You don't have to stop," he said.

"I know. But Mama—" Campbell let the word trail off. Lacey wondered if Campbell thought Grandmother would throw up a blockade and run out and grab them as they drove by.

"Do you always refer to it as Mama's, never Papa's?" David asked. "I notice it was your father who aligned them up together yesterday."

"Yeah," Lacey said, remembering how she felt like the center dot on the five-side of a domino.

Campbell shrugged. "That's just because he knew what she was thinking. They always back each other up. That's good, I guess."

"Not if one of them is wrong," David said. "I hate it when parents back each other up just to have a united front, even when the front is wrong."

"Yeah," Lacey said, grinning.

"Besides," David said, "I consider people weak, not strong, when they can't stand it unless everyone does things their way."

"Yeah," Lacey said again.

Campbell gave her a playful tap on the head and said, "Oh, you."

By nightfall, however, Campbell and David were presenting a united front against her. They wanted to go to the folk dancing over at the Craft School and said she must come, too.

26

"I hate dancing," she said. She *was* rope, not lace, she thought. She could run and stomp and kick, but she didn't glide very gracefully.

"You can just sit and watch," David said. "No one will make you dance if you don't want to."

She couldn't imagine anything more boring. "But I stayed home alone in Colorado."

Even before Campbell said, "This isn't Colorado," Lacey knew the reason.

"I'm not afraid of my grandmother," she said.

"That isn't the point at all, David said. "We're in a new place and we're not used to things yet."

Yeah, she thought. Especially forceful grandmothers. "So, what are you doing, David? Keeping a united front?"

"Lacey, get your butt up and come on," he said, and he and Campbell headed out the door.

"Oh, allll right," she said, and trailed behind them. From the truck, she looked back at the house. One lone light shined out into the barren dark. She wasn't the scared type, but she realized she didn't know the lights and shadows of this house yet, or the creaks it made. She was relieved they had made her come. Even so, she said, "I don't see why I have to come," and she slumped down in the seat to prove she meant it.

Though they arrived almost on the dot of the appointed time, hardly anyone was there. A woman in an ankle-length tiny-print dress with a deep ruffle at the bottom stood in a corner with her back to the door. Near her, several musicians were tuning up on a stage. There was a violin and a cello and a couple of instruments Lacey didn't recognize, one a stringed instrument and one more like a clarinet than anything else she knew. The woman turned and it was Ms. Lamb, who greeted them with the same enthusiasm she had two days before.

"I haven't seen a dulcimer in years," Campbell said, walking right over to the musicians. Ms. Lamb introduced them and a man named Matthew handed Campbell the narrow stringed instrument. Campbell hugged it to herself and began strumming.

"I didn't know you could play anything," Lacey said.

"Sure," Campbell said, smiling in some new way. For just a moment, Lacey had that feeling of loss again.

"And a recorder," Campbell said, handing back the dulcimer and stroking the polished wood of the clarinet-type instrument.

"That's a recorder?" Lacey said, looking at David. She'd had a recorder in sixth grade music in Colorado. It was a red plastic whistle, a children's toy. David shrugged, but what she'd wanted from him was not an explanation of the instrument, but an explanation of her divided mother. She had only known a part of Campbell, the Colorado part. David and Campbell had both kept so quiet about their pasts.

"It's a tenor recorder," Matthew said, playing such rich, vibrant tones that Lacey thought this must be the sort of "pipe" the Pied Piper played to lure all those children. The sound was hypnotic. She would follow him anywhere, especially away from this strange new Campbell.

Patricia Lamb announced the first dance. Lacey turned and was surprised to see that enough people had come in to start the dance.

David held a hand out to Campbell. "I trust you won't mind if I make a fool of myself," he said.

"I'm sure you won't," Campbell said. "But if you do, I won't mind."

"You next," David said to Lacey.

She shoved her hands in her jeans pockets and shook her head and sidled to one of the chairs that lined the wall. She was not willing to make a fool of herself. She sat self-consciously at first, afraid someone might try to make her dance. Ms. Lamb explained the steps and had the dancers practice each sequence before she put on the music. David made missteps and turned wrong ways and Campbell whirled him back the right way and they were both laughing by the time the dance was over.

Lacey was not laughing. Uh-uh, she thought. There was no way she was getting out there. More people came in and some of them sat down to watch, too, so she wasn't the only one sitting. She began to relax a little and to notice people. David, Campbell, and some others were in jeans. Two of the men were in old faded overalls as though they'd just come in from the field. Most of the women had on dresses or skirts that flared gracefully with every turn. Several men had on polyester slacks and a few women had on ordinary skirts and wore panty hose. Even the shoes were interesting, everything from brogans and sneakers to dancing slippers. She made a game of trying to pair people up, but once a dance began, everyone was all mixed up again.

The faces were just as varied as the clothes. Women wore makeup or none and had hair carefully done or hanging straight or unceremoniously clipped up on the head. Men had short hair or long, beards or none and the beards were either manicured or scraggly.

Suddenly a yellow-haired girl was in front of her, taking her hands.

"Hey! You're here. Why aren't you dancing?"

Lacey blinked and pulled her hands loose.

The girl took hold of them again and shook them. "I'm Tam," she said.

"Tam!" Lacey had forgotten to look for Tam. Over Tam's shoulder, she saw two smaller replicas holding hands on the dance floor. Next to them was Kenny with a larger model.

"Come on, dance," Tam said, still shaking Lacey's hands.

Lacey shook her head, glad to be sturdy enough so that Tam, for all her tugging, couldn't budge her from the chair. She almost laughed at the hands going up and down and her head going side to side. "I'm Lacey," she said, staring at this scrawny blond cousin.

"I know that," Tam said, still pumping and pulling the hands. "Come on. It's fun."

Lacey kept shaking her head, a bit enchanted with Tam's skin, so fair and thin she could see the track of blue vein from the side of the eye into the hairline.

"Okay, then shove over and I'll sit with you."

30

Lacey thought there might be room for two Tams on the chair but not a Tam and a Lacey, but she shoved over, bracing a foot on the floor to keep from falling.

"Seems like I've waited all my life to meet you," Tam said.

"Me, too," Lacey replied, although she hadn't known it until that moment. They sat, bodies pressed together, Tam fully on the chair and swinging her feet just as she had recently been swinging Lacey's hands.

"That's a contra, when they line up like that with the men on one side and the women on the other," Tam said. Line was "lan," and like and life had come out "lak" and "laff." It reminded Lacey of how she'd enjoyed David's accent when they'd first met him. He'd lost it now, along with those parts of his past he didn't speak of.

"Sometimes we do square dances, sometimes round. You know. A circle. See that man in the overalls? Isn't he about the skinniest bean you ever saw?"

Lacey smiled at a skinny bean calling another bean skinny. The overalls were so loose it was as though they were empty, even with the man inside.

"That's Harris. Daddy don't like him. Daddy thinks he's a wimp."

Lacey shrank from the description and studied the man. He was tall, a much longer bean than Tam, and he dipped and bobbed as he danced. His gray hair was pulled into a ponytail and his beard could have been. She wondered what Kenny thought a wimp was.

"Daddy don't like beards," Tam said.

Ah, Lacey thought. Kenny thought a man with a beard was a wimp. She shrugged. She looked at Kenny, her Uncle Kenny, who was dark-haired and heavy-boned like David and the Bittners. Clunky as he was, he moved smoothly as he stepped toward Marlene, then away, and turned her under his arm. Lacey liked him. The Tam replicas were not quite as graceful as Kenny and Marlene, but they were as lithe as willows. Watching all these people do something she couldn't do made her feel cumbersome. She swung her free foot and kicked her heel against the rung of the chair. Well, there were things she could do that they couldn't, she bet.

She looked at Tam and asked, "Can you make a nail?"

Tam said, "Huh?"

Sunday Dinner

BY SUNDAY MORNING, IT WAS COLDER INSTEAD OF warmer, so dinner was set up inside at Kenny's instead of outside on the boardwalk. Greetings that had been exchanged at the dance the night before were repeated. Lacey had to remind herself that when people said "Ann," they meant Campbell.

Marlene had her thin hair poked on top of her head and the three girls had theirs pulled back into ponytails. The girls, who had been so bold last night at the dance, hung back shyly here in their own house. Lacey tried not to stare at the yellow hair and the slender bones. Without really having considered it, Lacey had assumed her cousins would look like her, as she looked like Campbell and Campbell looked like Kenny and they all looked like Grandmother and Grandfather.

"Tam, Tina, Teresa, come on out from behind your mama and be friendly to your kin," Kenny said.

"Hello, Lacey. Hello, Aunt Ann," Tam said softly. No sound came from the other two but Lacey could tell from the way they moved their lips they meant to say, "Hey."

"Hello Tam, Tina, Teresa," Lacey said a bit too loudly, reminding herself of Ms. Lamb. She could scarcely believe these were the girls who had danced with no shy bones.

"Just call me Campbell," Campbell said.

"Campbell? What kind of name is that?" Kenny asked.

"Tomato, vegetable, chicken noodle," Grandmother said, coming into the room. "You know, soup."

The Tam-Tina-Teresa cousins giggled.

"It's the name I was given, Kenny Tom," Campbell said.

"All right, all right," Kenny said, shaking a finger at his daughters as they laughed some more. "You will call her Aunt Campbell. And don't let me hear you calling me Kenny Tom, you hear?"

"Lacey put her most solemn look on her face, nodded, and said, "I promise I won't, Uncle Kenny Tom."

"You!" he said, turning the pointing finger on her. She noticed his nails and knuckles were still outlined in black, and that surprised her. After Goop and scrubbing, David's hands were always clean.

"Hello, Uncle David," said the youngest girl, Teresa. She pronounced it Day-vid and pulled a loose strand of hair across her cheek and put it in her mouth.

"He's just David," Marlene said quickly, also using the American pronunciation. "He's not your uncle."

"Yet," Kenny said, winking and clasping David's hand as though they shared some secret. "And it's Dah-veed. Now let's eat. I'm starved."

"Dah-veed. What kind of name is that?" Marlene said, and the little girls giggled again. She waved an arm toward the kitchen corner of the large room they were in. "You'uns just help yourselves. Ann, you and Lacey start. You're the guests of honor. Just dip from the stove. Everyone but Teresey's big enough to hep hissef."

Campbell didn't move, so Lacey nudged her and walked around her and picked up a plate. Today, she noticed, no one was wearing red.

At the table, she hesitated a moment, wondering where to sit. There were four chairs on each side and one on each end. She left the end ones for Kenny and Marlene, and set her plate down at one of the middle places on one side. It would be fun to be surrounded by relatives. Campbell came up and sat opposite her, and David, with a wink at Lacey, took the middle place next to Campbell. Suddenly the table seemed as long and broad as the Mississippi, but quickly the cousins surrounded her. Tam sat on her left, Tina left of Tam, and Teresa on the end at her right. Grandfather took the end by Campbell and Grandmother stood balancing her plate in the air.

"Is it a law the children all sit on one side?" Grandmother asked. Except for the end chairs, which everyone seemed to be saving for Kenny and Marlene, the only place left was next to David. "Teresa, you get up and swap places with me."

"I want to sit here," Teresa said.

"I might need to help her with something, Mama," Marlene said, approaching that end of the table and sitting down between Teresa and Grandfather.

"You heard Grandmom," Kenny said, plunking his plate down at the other end. "Get your butt up and come around here. You need help with anything, I'll do it." Lacey was startled to hear Kenny use "butt" the same way David did. She glanced at Teresa. The child had hair in her mouth again, or still, and was looking at Marlene. "Don't look to your mama," Kenny said. "You heard me. Git."

"Come on over here by me," said David, smiling down the table at Teresa. "I need a blond next to me." Teresa slipped down and picked up her plate.

Marlene took the plate from her. "We'll pass it down, honey." Assembly-line fashion, Teresa's plate, glass of tea, silverware, and napkin were passed down the table while Grandmother's table setting traveled the other way. Grandmother settled in by Lacey, and Lacey wanted to shout or cry a protest for Teresa. She looked across at David and Campbell, but Campbell was scrutinizing her food and David was talking to Teresa, thrusting his fork to emphasize words. Good old David, she thought, smiling at this familiar mannerism. Glancing around the table, she saw the others were talking and eating as though nothing had happened. Even Marlene. How could Marlene squash her feelings like that? Lacey wondered. And if Grand-mother thought it was terrible to sit by David, then why would she make the youngest, baby grandchild do so?

Amid her thoughts and the table chatter, Lacey realized Tam was saying something to her.

"What?" she asked, turning and looking at this age-mate cousin.

"Look," Tam said. Tam was looking down, holding something in her hand. It was a photograph of two chubby babies, one grinning, one solemn; one with dark hair, one with light. "That's us," Tam said.

Lacey knew it was. She recognized herself from her baby pictures, but she was surprised to see that Tam had ever been chubby.

"See? I have been waiting all my life to meet you."

The strange sounds of some of the words—Tam's "laff," Marlene's "hep hissef"—and others clanged harshly on her ears. But the feeling of having kin softened everything.

Ridgewire

AS THEY WALKED OUT TO THE TRUCK TO HEAD FOR school on Monday, here came Grandmother up the drive-way with a car full of cousins.

"Is Lacey ready for school?" Grandmother asked, low-ering the electronic window of her blue-gray Buick. Lacey looked down at herself to see if anything about her looked unready.

"What're you doing here so bright and early?" David asked. It was not bright. Mist hung in the hair like trillions of spiderwebs. As if Lacey could read minds, she knew Campbell was thinking, What are you doing here, period.

"Well, Soup, I've come to get Lacey for school," Grandmother said. "I take the girls. Marlene has to be at work at seven, you know."

Campbell opened the passenger door of the truck. "No, Mama, I didn't know. School buses still run, don't they?"

"Yes, of course," Grandmother said, "but it's just as easy for me to take them. Just like I did you young'uns."

Lacey was thinking it wasn't all that easy, two miles winding in the opposite direction.

"That's a flat-out lie, Mama," Campbell said. Lacey looked at Campbell with a start. "You had no interest whatsoever in carrying me to school until someone else was interested in taking me."

"Come on, Lacey," Tam said. "Come with us and Grandmom."

"Thanks just the same, Eva," David said, "but we have to get her registered." Now Lacey looked at David, surprised to hear him call Grandmother Eva. She shrugged. She guessed he wouldn't call her Grandmother or Mama, and Mrs. Bittner would sound a bit stiff. One thing David wasn't was stiff.

"Well, sakes, don't you think I know how to register a child for school? Who do you think got Teresa here registered? And Tina, too? I took them just like they were my own," Grandmother said. "Well, they are my own. And you are, too, Lacey Ann."

"Lacey who?" Lacey said.

"All of us better get along," David said.

"Ohhhh, come ride with us," Tam said. "Grandmom, make her come with us."

David climbed into the truck and Campbell held the passenger door for Lacey.

"I'll see you at school," Lacey said to Tam, her back teeth clenched a little over the "make her" remark. "What did Grandmother call me?" she asked when she was in the truck. David waited for Grandmother to turn around. Grandmom, the cousins called her.

"She wanted you named Lacey Ann instead of Lacey Campbell."

Lacey looped an arm through Campbell's and squeezed. "I'm glad you got your way." She liked her name, Lacey Campbell Bittner. She liked it that she, her mother, and her grandmother all had the name Campbell, which had been Grandmother's maiden name.

Campbell squeezed back and laughed, as David followed Grandmother down and out of the driveway. "I occasionally got my way," she said, "but never without a fight."

Grandmother poked along the narrow curvy road. There was no place to pass until after Bitter Creek.

"Does she always drive this slowly?" David asked.

"Only when she wants to aggravate someone," Campbell said.

On a straight stretch just past the turnoff to the barn, David passed Grandmother and drove at normal speed. She immediately speeded up and kept pace, all the way to the schoolyard in Savory.

"Now, you see, Asparagus?" Grandmother said, zizzing down the electronic window as she pulled up beside them in the parking lot. "I could have just as well brought her and saved you the trouble."

"Lacey is never any trouble for us," David said.

The remark made Lacey feel treasured. She climbed down out of the truck. The cousins hopped out of the Buick and Tam took hold of Lacey's hand again.

"You have always been the most stubborn girl in five counties," Grandmother said to Campbell.

"Reckon where I got that from," Campbell said.

"I could have seen to her registration," Grandmother said. Lacey and Tam looked at one another and grinned, as though this adult silliness bonded them even more than being cousins. "You don't even know where the office is."

"I'll show you," Tam said to Lacey.

David grinned broadly, leaned into Grandmother's open window and said, "You know what, Eva? I'll bet we can find it." Grandmother buzzed the window shut in his face and David laughed. But Grandmother and Campbell were grim-lipped.

"I'm glad you are quick," Lacey said to David. "She almost got your nose."

"We'll melt her," he said, touching his nose as if to be certain it was still there. "We'll melt her."

Inside the school was dark and dreary, completely different from the bright glass and chrome school Lacey had attended in Colorado. The bulletin board had notices stuck up just any old way, with no special touches to make it attractive.

"Try to get in my class," Tam said, leaving them at the office door. "Mrs. Davis."

"Ann Bittner," said a very tall man as soon as they entered the office. "I've been watching for you." The man looked past Lacey to David. "Though, obviously, you're not Ann Bittner anymore."

"Fred?" Campbell said. "Fred Palmer?"

"Yes, it's me."

Campbell laughed. "Are you principal here?" When he nodded, she said, "I wonder why Mama didn't tell me?" He shrugged. "How did you know to look for me?" she asked.

"Ridgewire," he said.

"Then you know I'm still a Bittner. The name that's changed is the first one. I dropped the Ann. I'm Campbell Bittner. This is David Habib." Campbell extended an arm back toward David and David stepped forward and shook hands with Fred Palmer. "And this is Lacey." Campbell placed a hand on Lacey's shoulder. "You remember Lacey."

The man reached out and touched both of her shoulders. "Yes, of course, I do. Lacey, we're glad to have you back in Bitter Creek."

"Thank you," Lacey said, looking way up to see his face. It was strange to be welcomed back to a place she never remembered being in. "Can I be in Mrs. Davis's class?"

"Now I wonder why you're asking that," he said. "Don't you think it will be confusing, two Bittners in the same class?"

"I don't see why," Lacey said. "We don't look a thing

alike and I promise not to write Tam's name on my paper to try to fool the teacher."

"I see you have your father's sense of humor," Fred Palmer said.

Lacey looked quickly at Campbell and stepped back to link her arm through David's. "Does he know my father?" she asked Campbell.

"Yes," Campbell said.

Lacey swallowed hard. Here it was, this thing she so seldom thought about, this thing that had nothing to do with her life. "I have David's sense of humor," she said.

"No, indeed, Old Lace," David said. "You have your very own."

"Sorry if I said anything I shouldn't," Fred Palmer said.

"Oh, no, she knows all about it," Campbell said. "Lacey, Mr. Palmer is Wally's brother."

Lacey's mouth opened and air rushed in. Palmer, Palmer, Wally Palmer. Wally was her father.

"Well, it's Tam's class for you, then," tall Palmer said. David and Campbell blew her a kiss and she followed Mr. Palmer down the hallway. The door where Mr. Palmer stopped was labeled Ms. Davis.

When she walked into the room, she saw Tam immediately and Tam's mouth made a round "oh" of silent delight. The room was bright and cheerful, not drab like the hallway outside the office. She was introduced and shown to a desk. As she sat she thought Palmer, Palmer. She had almost forgotten her father's name was Palmer.

"Lacey Bittner."

Lacey looked up, startled, then realized it was only roll call and her name had been added. She couldn't keep the names of her new classmates straight, but she and Tam smiled and waved across the room. Announcements were made, one about a sixth-grade bake sale and another about something called flag corps. Several nearby students whispered cheerful, welcoming things. Others smiled shyly. There was a comfortable atmosphere in the room, as though you could speak out without having your head chopped off. Lacey wiggled to be more at ease in her desk, and she looked around. Her eyes landed on a boy two rows over, rather, on his hair, which was fiery red and stuck out like porcupine quills.

His eyes bounded back, glaring, wild as his hair. "What rock did you crawl out from under?" he hissed.

Lacey almost laughed. He'd stepped into a trap and she hadn't even set one. Colorado was rock country. She might not have learned the names of wildflowers, and she didn't really know much about rocks, but she knew the four basic groups.

"An extrusive igneous one," she said.

The nearby classmates giggled.

"Well-l-ll," the boy said. Beneath the shock of hair, his scalp turned red, as if by reflection. "Well-l-ll," he said, the punch gone out of his voice. "You should have stayed there."

That afternoon, Lacey babbled about school. After Campbell laughed with appreciation about "extrusive

44

igneous," Lacey said, "Tell me about my father."

"You know all that," Campbell said.

Yes, she did. Her mother and Wally were sweethearts who broke up and afterwards Campbell, who was called Ann then, found out she was pregnant. The Bittner and Palmer parents wanted them to get married, but Wally was already going with someone else and Campbell had already decided that Wally was not who she wanted to marry. Wally said he would marry her if that's what she wanted, but she didn't think a wrong marriage would do either them or the baby any good.

"I don't mean all that," Lacey said. "I mean, is my father tall?" That wasn't what she meant, either, but she didn't know what she meant.

"Yes." Campbell laughed. "You could never miss either Palmer coming or going."

Lacey fidgeted. She was uncomfortable asking, because of David, even though he wasn't here. Not that he minded. She was the one who minded. David was so much her father, so much like the father she wanted. She had never missed her blood father. Tony and Ralph, and now David, had been enough.

"Where does he live?" she asked.

"In Asheville," Campbell said.

Lacey relaxed a little. At least he didn't live here. Asheville was enough mountain-miles away to keep him safely out of her life, as he had been. He was nothing to her, just someone Campbell had known once.

"Is he one of the ones who wanted to take you to school?"

Campbell smiled. "Yes," she said. "And he did, too."

"Does he know we're back?"

"I don't know, sweetheart. But he will."

Lacey grimaced. "Yeah. I guess Mr. Palmer will tell him."

"That, or ridgewire," Campbell said.

"Mr. Palmer said that this morning. What's ridgewire?"

Campbell laughed again. "This is a small place, Lacey. I hope you won't find it too difficult. Anything that happens, everyone knows. The news travels across the ridges faster than any telephone wire. If there was not a single phone in the county, and I stopped to pick daisies one day on the way into town, the town would know about it before I got there. That's ridgewire."

Choices

THE NEXT MORNING, AS LACEY WALKED DOWN THE driveway to wait for the school bus, here came Grandmother and the cousins.

"Well, good morning," Grandmother said, zizzing down the car window. "I see we synchronized just right."

"I'm going to catch the school bus," Lacey said.

"Ohhh-hh," wailed Tam.

"You'll do no such of a thing," Grandmother said.

Lacey looked back toward the house, which was closed tight against the spring cold. Smoke plumed from the chimney and feathered up through the trees.

"Lacey Bittner, you get in this car," Grandmother said.

"I, uh, forgot one of my books," Lacey said. As she turned and walked back up the driveway, Grandmother drove along beside her, gravel crunching and popping beneath the tires.

"Lacey, what in the world?" Campbell said when Lacey returned to the house. David was washing the breakfast dishes and Campbell was drying and they were kissing between every dish.

Lacey pointed toward the front of the house. David took the dish towel from Campbell and dried his hands as they all three walked through the living room.

"Well, I'll be," David said when he looked out the window.

"Ohhh-hh," Campbell said, sounding like Tam.

"Campbell, you stay here," David said. "Come on, Old Lace." He walked her out past Grandmother's car. "Morning, Eva. Girls. Lacey's going to ride the bus if it's all the same to you."

"No, it's not all the same to me," Grandmother said from behind them. "Where's chicken-and-rice?" They heard the car backing and turning, then coming down the driveway. "Some people don't know how to let anybody do them a favor," Grandmother said.

"It has to be something you want done for it to be a favor, Eva," David said.

"Ohhh-hh," Tam wailed. Tina only stared, and Teresa looked like she was about to cry.

Lacey heard the uphill pull of a heavy motor. "Here comes the bus," she said.

48

"Run along, Old Lace," David said, giving her an affectionate smack on the bottom.

She just reached the end of the driveway when the yellow whale of a bus stopped and the doors opened with a hydraulic hiss. Lacey scampered aboard and glanced back at the Buick, waiting to pounce from the end of the driveway. From behind it, David waved.

"Welcome aboard," the young bus driver said. "You just did make it."

"I know," she said as the doors sighed closed. She felt protectively swallowed up into this busload of people. As she settled herself into the first available seat, she wondered if Jonah had found comfort in the warm, enclosed space of the whale's belly. The bus lurched forward and she avoided looking back, but in a moment and right in a curve, Grandmother whizzed past.

"Isn't that your grandmother?" someone behind her asked. "Does she always drive that fast?"

Only when she wants to provoke someone, Lacey thought, knowing exactly who it was Grandmother wanted to provoke. She turned to look at the speaker. How did this stranger know the woman in the car was her grandmother? Ridgewire?

"You're the new girl in Mrs. Davis's class," the girl said. More yellow hair, but this girl was larger than Tam and quite mature in the chest.

"Ms. Davis?" Lacey asked.

"Mrs., Ms., what's the difference?"

Lacey shrugged. The difference, she thought, was in

being called what you wanted to be called.

"Yeah. I saw you yesterday. My name is Shirl."

"Yeah, I saw you, too," Lacey said, remembering. "You're the one who made the announcement about flag corps practice."

"Yeah," Shirl said. "My mother's in charge of flag corps. You're coming out, aren't you? Everybody does. All the girls, I mean."

Lacey shrugged as the bus passed between the two Bittner buildings in Bitter Creek. There was the blue-gray Buick parked in front of the Gas and Gro. So much for being in such an all-fired hurry, she thought.

"So, Mr. Palmer is your uncle, huh?" Shirl said.

Lacey bit her bottom lip with her teeth. Ridgewire had made it to the school bus. "You might say that," she said.

"Might say? What does that mean?" Shirl asked. "Either he is your uncle or he isn't, right?" The bus had stopped again and the greetings of boarding students interrupted the direction of the conversation. They were back to flag corps.

"You're going to join, aren't you?" the newcomers asked Lacey. Their own chatter saved her from having to answer Shirl. Everyone, apparently, did join, but she had never been inclined to do what everyone did.

"We sixth graders practice this last month of school so we'll be ready when junior high starts in the fall," Shirl explained.

Junior high, Lacey thought as the bus jounced along. She hardly had time to get used to this new school before summer. It seemed strange and a little lonely to already be thinking of another new one in the fall.

Though Lacey hadn't seen Grandmom's car again, Tam was already at school, watching for Lacey's bus.

"You're going to join, aren't you?" Tam asked, running up and grabbing hold of Lacey's hand. "Seems like I've waited my whole life to be in flag corps." Lacey smiled. Tam, it seemed, had been waiting her whole life for lots of things. "Did you bring your permission slip? You can ride with me and Grandmom." They just don't know, Lacey thought, how stubborn I am when people try to tell me what to do. They entered the building and the classroom and Tam ran up to the teacher's desk with her own permission slip. Like the others, Tam forgot to notice that Lacey hadn't answered.

When the bell rang, those not already in their seats scampered to them. As Lacey sat, she felt something beneath her. She brushed the seat and jumped, startled, when her hand touched something small and soft. The girls in the next row squealed. She looked and saw a mouse.

Quickly, she cupped it in her hands, then discovered it was made of felt.

"It was Bradley," one of the girls said, pointing to a boy two rows over. It was him, with the escaping red hair. The girls made repulsive sounds and cringed from Lacey as she held it.

"It's only a mouse," she said, and drew more squeals when she leaned forward and threw it at Bradley. He was quick, and he caught it. Then he grinned at her.

"Okay, settle down back there," Ms. Davis said. "Bradley, if you keep bringing that mouse to school, I will have to put it on the roll."

Lacey smiled. She liked this Ms. Davis. Some teachers would have stomped down the aisle and seized the mouse. As Ms. Davis began to call the roll, Lacey looked around, trying to learn the names of her other classmates. Bradley was looking at her. He had a million freckles and his hair was, she decided, the color of the flame azalea.

For fourteen school days, Grandmother appeared in the driveway every morning. That was two more Saturday nights of watching folk dances, two more Sunday dinners at Kenny's, and lots of daylight savings evenings at the barn.

David tried to encourage her to dance, and when she wouldn't, he said, "Okay, Lace. You tell me when you're ready."

On Sundays, Grandmom was one of the first to fill her plate so she could watch for a seat that would not be next to David.

At the barn, David had hauled in a truckload of gravel to make a base area for his forge.

The junior high, and the high school, too, were right there on the same campus as the elementary school, so it wouldn't be such a change. Bradley had become her friend as well as Shirl. She'd learned that Shirl was really Cheryl, the Appalachian tongue cutting off a syllable. And certain Appalachian tongues—some of her classmates, some of her family—angled off words. "Fire," "bear," "square," and "hair" were all pronounced to rhyme with "car." But the word "quarry" was said "queery."

Tam had joined flag corps and begged Lacey to join. Lacey even watched for a while one afternoon when Campbell was picking her up. The flash of flags, medium blue and gold, was beautiful. But moving in precision with dozens of other people wasn't her idea of fun.

"Tam keeps pestering me about flag corps and riding with Grandmom," Lacey complained to Campbell. The "Grandmom" was beginning to come out of her mouth easily, since it's what the cousins put in her ear.

"Well, you'll just have to handle it," Campbell said. "Or do you want to move back to Colorado?"

"What?" Lacey said, her feelings sloshing at the abrupt turn. Colorado was home. But cousins were here. "Is David thinking about going back?"

"No, he's not. But we could go back."

Campbell's words froze Lacey's windpipe. Even more than Colorado, David was home. She tried to swallow, and the trickle of saliva thawed her throat a bit. "Are you thinking about it?" she asked, managing to push a whisper up through the ice. Numbers of times through the years they had made hasty moves, but none between such distances as here and Colorado, except that first one, which was before memory.

"No, but it is a choice. We can either go back or we can stay here and handle whatever comes. But that means you have to handle whatever comes to you."

"Well, golleee," Lacey said, using sass to cover her fear.

53

"I never asked you to handle anything. I was just talking. Can't I even talk?"

"Oh, Lacey, yes. Of course." Campbell reached out and pulled Lacey into a hug, rubbed her hair, and kissed her head. "I'm just so scared."

"I know," Lacey said. But suddenly, with Campbell admitting fear, she was no longer afraid, as though Campbell could be afraid enough for both of them. "But there's no reason to be. She's not going to kidnap me."

"Oh, baby, I know. But I was so happy in Colorado." Campbell finished the embrace and Lacey stepped back.

"Aren't you happy here? David's here."

Campbell ran her finger along the floral design she had tooled into a belt. "I never learned how to be happy within a thousand miles of my mother," she said.

Lacey was flooded with relief that it wasn't that way with her. She was happy near her mother. But perhaps Campbell had been, too, when she was twelve. "Never?" she asked. "Not even when you were little?"

"Oh, I remember being proud as anything when they started letting me make change in the store." Campbell smiled. "I guess I was happy then."

"Well, what happened?" Lacey asked.

"Ohh, I started to grow up, I guess," Campbell said.

"When boys got interested in taking you to school?"

"I guess." Campbell laughed. "They didn't want me noticing boys or boys noticing me. They wanted to keep me locked up until I was fifty-two."

Lacey laughed, too, thinking of John, who'd sat in front

of her in school in Colorado and how she thought she'd remember forever the way every hair whorled out from a crown of cowlicks on the back of his head. Quite different from the way Bradley's sprang away. "But can't you be happy now?" she asked.

"I wish," Campbell said with a sigh. "But you've seen her in action, how she bullies everyone and expects them to comply. And they do, too. And now look at Tam. So quiet and shy-seeming. Just a wisp of a thing, all those girls. But Tam has Mama's ways, trying to bully you off the school bus."

Before Grandmom and Grandpop crossed the road to dinner on the fourth Sunday, Kenny joined in the pestering. "What would it hurt, Campbell, to let Mama carry Lacey back and to with the girls? What would it hurt to give her this pleasure in her old age?"

"Fifty is not exactly the grave, Kenny," Campbell said.

Fifty, Lacey thought, was half a century. It sounded pretty old to her.

"Well, you know, Mama likes to be the boss. But we pick and choose what we'll let her be the boss of," he said.

"Yes, I noticed," Campbell said, "and I don't like some of your choices."

"I don't know why you're still so resentful," Kenny said. "It's been ten years."

Campbell shook her head and watched Kenny scrape beneath his nails with his pocketknife. Lacey noticed that no matter how he scraped, the nails never seemed to come clean.

Kenny shrugged, folded the knife, and slid it into his pocket. "Well, it has been ten years," he said, "you're sure right about that."

"Who's right about what?" asked Grandmom, appearing in the doorway with Grandpop behind her.

"Right about here y'all come and let's eat," Kenny said quickly.

"Well, let's do. I see cream of mushroom is here," Grandmom said.

"That's getting pretty old, Mama," Campbell said.

"Do you prefer cream of onion? I named you Ann. I didn't intend for you to call yourself after a soup."

David winked at Lacey.

This time David was last to the table. Tam suddenly slid over and made a space between herself and Grandmom. David sat. Grandmom looked startled for a moment.

"Teresa," she said, standing up and picking up her plate.

Marlene already had a hand on Teresa's arm. "No, baby, you stay right where you're at."

"Marlene," Kenny said.

Lacey tried to be still enough to keep Teresa from moving.

In a voice as sweet as sourwood honey, Marlene said, "Kenny, why don't you swap places with your mama?"

Kenny bobbed this way and that for a moment, then picked up his fork and said, "Mama, why don't you just sit back down and let's all for godsakes eat."

Summer Roots

THE MOUNTAIN LAUREL BLOOMED. SCHOOL WAS OUT and immediately the days became too long for Lacey. David was teaching blacksmithing every day but Sunday and spending what little extra time he had at the barn. Campbell was doing leatherwork—belts, billfolds, even working on a saddle again—and spending what extra time she had at the barn. Tam was working at Bittner's stocking shelves, sweeping floors, waiting on customers inside and out, and sometimes taking care of Teresa.

"Come on over," Tam said twice a week from the pivotal points of folk dances and family dinners. Lacey wanted to see Tam, but she didn't want to go over there, across from the Gas and Gro. Even though Grandmom declared love, she had such a hateful attitude.

"I don't have any roots," she said, watching Campbell for a reaction, but Ms. Cool Cucumber Soup gave none.

"Sure you do," said David. "But even when you have roots, you have to nourish them yourself. And sometimes you have to make your own roots."

"How do you do that?" she asked.

"Well, right now you need summer roots," he said. "Think of things you'd like to do."

"That's the trouble," she said. She was at the end of liking the things she used to do—playing at something or nothing for hours, spending time with Campbell doing leatherwork or helping David at the forge. She was too old to play all day, and she already knew how to make a belt and a billfold, to fire the furnace and make a nail. Leatherwork or blacksmithing held no permanent interest for her.

"I miss the horses," she said. In Colorado, though they'd never had their own horse, the ones Campbell boarded and trained at a friend's ranch had seemed like their own. That was something she would like to do forever, board and train horses.

"Ah, Lacey, I know," David said. "But we just don't have a place for them. If I could only find some land to buy." She knew he meant, If I could only afford to buy some. She thought there was plenty around to buy, she saw FOR SALE signs everywhere.

"Can't you rent some, like you rent the barn?"

58

David laughed. Renting took "affording," too, she knew. Now she was sorry he'd been in such a hurry to set up his own shop. What fun it would be to be looking for a barn and building the forge now, in the long days of summer.

"Read," Campbell suggested.

"You read," she said back.

"I'm not the one who's bored," Campbell said.

"If you won't read, at least look," David said a few days later, and he handed her a book on wildflowers.

"Huh!" she said. Still, she looked up trillium. The blossoms were long gone, but the triplet leaves hovered protectively over the vacant pod. There were other kinds of trillium besides the nodding *Trillium cernuum,* she discovered, and she wished for spring back so she could see them. While Campbell worked at the side porch on the saddle, Lacey was in the woods near the house looking for wildflowers. It surprised her how hard it was to really see, to notice enough about what she was looking at to find it in the book, whether the leaves were alternate or opposite, lanceolate or oblong.

"I found pipsissewa," she said, running to tell Campbell every discovery. "It has spiky, pointed leaves and tiny, inside-out flowers that hang like bells." She showed Campbell the picture from the book.

"I know what it looks like, Lacey," Campbell said.

When David and Campbell were at the forge, Lacey was up in the cove or down beneath the fringe of thick trees that bordered the creek.

"I found Solomon's seal," she said, still announcing each find. "It has a long, arching stem of leaves and a row of delicate flowers hanging underneath."

"I know," Campbell said.

"Yes, you know the names of everything," Lacey said in disgust.

"Well, I don't," said David. He shoved the tongs, which held a hot stem of iron, toward Campbell, who automatically took it. "Why don't you show me?"

"David," Campbell protested.

"You can do that as well as I can," he said. "Well," he winked at Lacey, "almost as well." They were making the frame for a fire screen. When finished, it would have iron fronds of wild grasses across the front. In a stage whisper, pretending Lacey shouldn't hear, he said, "I think we've been ignoring the kid." He walked out with her and she showed him the Solomon's seal, and the way the trillium leaves were hugging the seed pod which was, she had learned, called the receptacle.

"Some of the words in this book are ridiculous," she said.

"Like what?"

"Glabrous. Sessile. Peduncle."

"What do they mean?"

"I don't know," she said.

Lowering himself to the creek bank, he broke off a blade of river cane and slid it between his thumbs. When he blew across it there was a piercing shriek.

"How do you do that?" she asked.

"You mean I haven't shown you?" He taught her how to place the blade between the incurves of her thumbs and use it as a reed. Soon she was duplicating the shrieking whistle.

Taking the book from her, he flipped toward the front and showed her a glossary that listed all the flowerly words used in the book. "Learn those three words for me by supper," he said. "Glabrous, sessile, and something like pet uncle."

Lacey giggled. "That must be Kenny. He's the only uncle I've got." The shadow of Fred Palmer passed through her mind and out into the air. He wasn't really an uncle. He didn't act like an uncle. She didn't think of him as an uncle.

"Do you wish we were still in Colorado?" he asked.

She put a finger in her mouth and ran the nail across the top ridges of her bottom teeth. "Sometimes," she said.

"I thought you'd like it here, with cousins and all."

Near her feet a salamander crawled out from under a rock.

"Since school's out, I don't even see Tam without everyone else around."

"Why don't you go see her, then?"

The salamander skimmed along a shallow where the water barely covered rock and sand.

"You know Campbell won't let me," she said, picking up a chunky rock and hurling it into the creek. It made a satisfactory *p-lump* and *sp-lash,* but the ripples vanished into the current.

"I've never heard her say such a thing," he said. He

picked up several small stones and volleyed them at Lacey's rock, which was clearly visible among all the others in the flux of crystal water.

"She doesn't have to say it. We all know it."

"No, we don't all know it," he said. "If you want to spend time with your cousin, you should make arrangements to do so. Quit making excuses for yourself. You're twelve years old."

"But, Campbell—" she began.

"But Campbell nothing, Lacey." He cut her off sharply. "Campbell has her own private war with the family, but it's not genetic. You don't have to inherit it unless you choose to. It's your life." He pinged a few more stones. "Do you know what I was doing when I was your age?"

She blinked. Yes. She did know. His parents had been brutally killed and he was living in a commune sort of place and was equally responsible with everyone else for everything involved in the life there—working, cooking, laundry, getting along. But that was another time and another country. What did it have to do with her? Besides, Campbell's problems with the family did have to do with her directly.

"You have to make your own happy endings, Lacey." David had stood up and now he walked away. She wanted to say something sharp and smart-alecky behind him, such as "How would you know?" but she knew he did know. The country he was from was Iran. One way he made his happy ending was by not mentioning it. He loved his native country, but there was such hatred toward Iran that when people knew where he was from, it immediately created a barrier.

Staring at the water, she no longer knew which rock she had thrown into the creek. She hefted another, but it didn't make much of a splash. In her mind's eye, she walked toward Bitter Creek.

With a clearness she didn't much like, she saw it was herself who wouldn't let her go alone to Bitter Creek. She had let herself inherit the family war.

At supper she announced, "The pet uncle is peduncle. It's the main stalk of a flower. You're my peduncle, David."

"What a lovely thing to say, Lacey," he said.

"Sessile is when a leaf or flower comes right off the peduncle without having a stem of its own."

"Then you're definitely not sessile," he said. "You have a strong stem of your own."

Campbell licked the moisture from the rim of her glass and smiled at the two of them.

"And on the palms of our hands and the bottoms of our feet," Lacey said, "we're all glabrous."

"What?" David said, laughing, pleased with the exchange, pleased she'd learned the words.

"Hairless," she said.

Flat Rock Days

ONE MORNING LACEY CALLED TAM. "WHY DON'T YOU come over? You're not working all the time, are you?"

"Of course not," Tam said. "I'm not working this morning. But I don't have anyone to carry me."

Lacey knew who would "carry" her if she'd only ask, but she was glad Tam didn't want to ask. She didn't want Grandmom's Buick gliding up this driveway one more time.

"You have legs, don't you?" Lacey asked.

"You mean walk?" Tam sounded as though it was fourteen miles.

"Yes," said Lacey, who had thought it out before she

picked up the telephone. "You start walking and I'll start walking and we'll meet in the middle."

There was a long pause before Tam said, "Welllll."

"I thought we were going to be friends," Lacey said.

"We are friends," Tam said in a shocked tone.

"I thought you'd waited all your life to meet me," Lacey said, and in spite of herself "life" came out "laff" and she knew she was mocking, not adapting. A ripple of shame pulsed through her.

"I have," Tam said in the same startled tone.

"Well, friends see each other," Lacey said. "I'm hanging up and starting to walk. When I figure I've gone halfway, I'll wait for you. If you don't come, I know we're really not friends." Still holding the receiver, she put her finger on the disconnect button and stood there waiting for the phone to ring back. It didn't. Watching the phone as though it might ring if she turned her back, she moved toward the porch.

"Campbell, I'm going halfway down the road to meet Tam and she's coming halfway to meet me, okay?" She was ready to be insistent, as she had been with Tam.

"Okay. That sounds like a good idea," Campbell said, looking up from where she was tooling an oak-leaf and acorn border on the saddle leather. "Be back for lunch, okay?"

Lacey turned and ran to make up for the time she had lost. As she walked along the road, her eyes gravitated to the wildflowers, and she was glad she'd brought the book. Maybe she and Tam could look at wildflowers together.

She wondered if Tam knew the names of everything.

She stopped to examine some tiny white flowers like four-pointed trumpets. Bright red flowers the size of a half dollar caused her to gasp in delight. She was tempted to stop to look these up, but she could not. Tam might be coming down the road. She ran again. The creek burbled and babbled over stones on her right and she kept her ears alert for the sound of cars. A fast driver coming around one of these curves could snap her off the side of the road in an instant. No cars came. The crisp mountain air penetrated to the far reaches of her lungs. In Colorado she'd had this sort of freedom, walking down the road to see her friends. Why had she thought she couldn't have it here? All Campbell had said was, "Be back for lunch, okay?"

Her stomach would have to tell her when that was, for she had no watch. She looked up, east. The sun was not long over the mountains and yet it was nearly ten. Perhaps she could tell noon by the sun. How, though, would she tell the halfway point along the road? Walking a mile ordinarily took her about fifteen minutes, but she had run and stopped and run some more, so time would be no judge even if she'd had a watch.

Then, hurrying from around the next curve came Tam, clutching her side. "Oh, Lacey Ann, you scared me half to death."

"What?" Lacey said, in response to what Tam had called her.

"Ohhhh. I have a stitch in my side," Tam said, leaning

into it. "I ran all the way. You scared me half to death saying we weren't friends."

"Well, you're here, so we are," Lacey said. "But what did you call me?" Tam looked blank. "You called me Lacey Ann."

"Well, it's your name, isn't it? What are we going to do now? Stand out in the road and visit?"

"No. Let's see if we can find a good spot by the creek." Lacey moved onto the shoulder of the road and picked her way through the scrubby growth. "And, no, it's not my name." A large flat rock jutted out into the creek, and Lacey stepped onto it.

"It's not?" Tam asked. "But Grandmom said—"

"Grandmom," Lacey said, "thinks she is boss of the near world. Including giving people new names if she doesn't like the one they have."

"Laceeeey, that's not very nice."

The girls settled onto the rock and Lacey squiggled to the edge, extending one leg to see if there was room to dangle both without wetting her shoes. There wasn't.

"Is it nice to change someone's name? Including calling Ms. Davis Mrs.?"

"Laceeey. She's married, Mrs. Davis is."

"What does that have to do with her name?" Lacey pulled off her sneakers and let her legs dangle. The first touch of water was a shock, but she didn't draw back.

"Lacey An—, uh, your feet are going to be purple in three seconds." Tam folded her legs and held her knees as though her feet might accidentally fall into the water. "If a woman is married, she is called Mrs."

"What's a name you hate, Tam?"

After thinking for a minute, Tam said, "Hortense."

"How would you like it if Grandmom called you Hortense?" Surely, she thought, Tam was smart enough to get the point.

"Well, what if Mrs. Davis wanted to be called Mr.? Would that be all right with you? Would you call her Mr.?"

"Sure I would, if that's what she wanted to be called," Lacey said, not at all sure she would, but unwilling to admit that Tam had a good comeback.

Piercing through the trees, the sun beamed onto the rock in one precise pillar of light. Tam moved into it and said, "Look, Lacey, I'm in the spotlight. Oh! Feel how warm the rock is here."

Lacey put her hand on the sunspot and absorbed the warmth. Every particle of moisture in the air was illuminated, giving the column of light the look of golden mist. Sitting beneath it, pale Tam had a luminous glow.

"Lacey," said the translucent Tam, "I don't know why you won't be friends with Grandmom."

Lacey splashed her feet. They had turned purple, then red, but were not quite used to the cold and were back to their normal color. Grandmom. She noticed Tam didn't say "and Grandpop," yet she was no more or less friendly with him. Grandpop almost disappeared into the background of Grandmom. This thought made Lacey curious about him. "Well," she said, "maybe there's a lot you don't know."

"Oh, I know all about that, how Campbell wouldn't let Grandmom help raise the baby. You, I mean. And got mad and left, and hardly ever let anyone know where you were."

"Somebody hasn't got the story straight," she said. "They tried to take me from her. They got a lawyer and tried to get legal custody."

"Lacey, that's a flat-out lie," Tam said.

Lacey winced from the way the accusation was expressed. Here was Tam using Campbell's phrase. Had that come from Grandmom, from Bitter Creek? Is that why Tam knew it? Was that a part of Tam's roots she shared?

"It's the flat-out truth," Lacey said, feeling all ten of the years of not being close to Tam.

"What's that book you have?" Tam asked.

Lacey was so lost in thought she almost didn't hear the question, almost didn't recognize that Tam was building a bridge across the gap.

"David gave it to me," she said, holding the book so Tam could see. "Do you know what that bright red flower is that looks like a fiery star?"

Tam shook her head and Lacey began thumbing through the book from the beginning. Just a few pages in, she found it.

"Look! Fire pink." She showed the picture to Tam. "Fire pink," she repeated. "It looks like starfire."

"I think I've seen it," Tam said.

Think, Lacey thought? How could you live in Bitter

Creek for twelve years and not be absolutely certain you'd seen this brilliant starfire? How could you live across the road from Grandmom for twelve years and not know the names of everything? She felt that she was, in this way, this love of wildflowers, closer to Grandmom than Tam was. Another piece of her roots. The sun was flooding the rock now and the column of mist was gone. Lacey pulled her feet out of the water.

"I guess I'd better go," she said. When she stood, her feet made damp footprints on the rock. "Campbell said for me to be home for lunch."

Tam looked worried. "Are we going to be friends?"

Lacey couldn't let herself lose a cousin she'd waited for all her life. "If you want," she said.

"Oh, I do," Tam said. Then she added Lacey's qualification. "If you want."

"I do," Lacey said.

"Promise?" Tam asked.

"I promise," Lacey said, and Tam took hold of Lacey's hands and shook them up and down.

They hugged briefly, then climbed the bank to the road. "This can be our special meeting place," Tam said.

"Yeah," Lacey said, liking the secluded secretness of it.

"We'll call it Flat Rock," Tam said. Lacey grinned. As they turned to walk opposite ways on the road, Tam asked, "What is your name, anyway, if it's not Lacey Ann?"

"Lacey Campbell," Lacey said. "Lacey Campbell Bittner."

"Oh," Tam said. "You're a soup, too."

70

Lacey laughed and kept laughing as she skipped down the road. "I am soup," she thought. "I am green pea. I am turkey noodle. I am tomato and rice!" She picked a bouquet of daisies and starfires and took them home to Campbell.

"Oh, fire pinks," Campbell said.

Lacey said, "I know," and she laughed and laughed.

The Wildflower Connection

THE TINY FOUR-POINTED TRUMPETS WERE SUMMER bluets. They didn't announce themselves boldly like fire pinks or Queen Anne's lace. To Lacey, because she had to look closely, they were especially beautiful. She lugged the wildflower book to the meetings at Flat Rock, learning coreopsis and butterfly milkweed along the way.

Since Tam had run all the way that first day, she really had to come farther, but she spurned Lacey's suggestion that they find a place more nearly halfway.

"No, Flat Rock is perfect," Tam said. And it was. They liked meeting in the morning when the sun bore down like pillars that propped up the sky. They lay on their stomachs to warm their backs and watched salamanders in a shallow rivulet that rambled into the creek. They named the salamanders Alexander, Sally, Alex, and Mandy.

"Ohhh-hh," Tam cried, pointing. A large Alexander had taken a small Alex into its mouth head first. Lacey reached down and grabbed the tail of each. "Ohhh-hh," Tam cried again when only half of the Alex came free. With a shudder of horror, Lacey dropped both tails. Scarcely blinking at the interruption, the larger salamander resumed his meal. With a gulp, gulp, gulp, the last bit of the small tail disappeared and there was only one fat Alexander squatting in the shallows. Both girls grimaced and sat up so they couldn't see the four-inch fiend.

"I didn't know they were cannibals," Tam said.

"I wonder why they are?" Lacey said.

Tam shrugged. "Mother Nature."

"Yes, but most of nature doesn't consume its own kind. I wonder why some do."

Tam shrugged again. "I don't like some of the ways of Mother Nature."

Lacey leaned over and saw the fat Alexander still there. She reached out and touched it. He scooted beneath a rock and she was glad to have it gone. She didn't want to see it there looking pregnant, not because it was going to birth a baby, but because it just ate one.

"I wonder if all fish are cannibals," she said. She recalled a Colorado friend whose parent guppies had gobbled up the babies.

"Who cares?" Tam said. "Just as long as they don't eat us."

"I just want to know everything. Don't you?"

Tam looked as though Lacey had said something very strange. "No," she said. Then Lacey looked as though Tam was the strange one. They burst out laughing.

Lacey tapped her wildflower book. "I need a book on salamanders," she said. She plucked a smooth, yellow stone from the water. "And one on rocks."

Tam shook her head, then nodded as a tiger butterfly drifted past. "And one on butterflies."

"Yes."

"And trees." Tam made a small sweep of her arm.

"Yes."

"And the sky," Tam said with a larger sweep.

"Yes."

"And the whole universe." This time she swept both arms, raising them together in front of her face, extending them above her head, then pushing them outward and down at full reach.

"You look like you're doing *Swan Lake*," Lacey said.

"What's that?" Tam asked, repeating the motions.

"It's a ballet," Lacey said. "About a swan."

Tam let her arms flow into the movements of a swan's neck and wings, arms rising as the mist evaporated into the sunbeams.

As June passed into July, Flat Rock days became the focal point of Lacey's week. Saturday night dances and Sunday dinners with the family fit in between.

The more wildflower names she learned, the more she

thought about Grandmom. This wildflower connection seemed stronger and even more important than sharing the names of Campbell and Bittner, or even being kin.

She surprised herself by announcing to Campbell, "Today, after Flat Rock, I think I'll walk to Grandmom's with Tam." She watched Campbell carefully for a reaction, but saw none. She surprised Tam even more, with her announcement. Tam almost fell off Flat Rock.

Tam took a long breath and held it. When she let it out, she asked, "What made you decide?"

Lacey held up the wildflower book. "I want to know the names of everything."

As they walked along, they sang silly songs. They laughed to think that in Colorado and North Carolina they'd learned some of the same ones. At Bitter Creek, as Lacey headed toward the store, Tam grabbed her hand.

"I have to let Daddy know I'm back," Tam said.

"Okay. I'll see you later," Lacey said.

"No-o-o," Tam wailed, tugging Lacey toward the garage. "Come with me for a minute. I want to see her face when she sees who's come."

In the garage, a pair of legs stuck out from under a pickup truck. Lacey assumed they were Kenny's.

"Daddy, I'm home," Tam said.

"Hey, baby," Kenny said. "Did you have a good time? Now you git on over there and relieve your grandmom of those young'uns."

"Yes, sir," Tam said to Kenny. To Lacey, she made a face and mouthed the words, "I always do."

"And bring me my lunch as soon as you can, sweetheart."

"I always do," Tam mouthed to Lacey.

"I'm about to starve," Kenny added.

"He always is," Tam whispered.

"What's that?" Kenny asked.

"Lacey's here," Tam said.

"Well, hello there, Lacey Campbell Bittner," Kenny said. "I thought Tam had sprouted another set of legs. It'd be good to see you if I could see you, but I can't let go of what I've got a holt of right now."

Lacey leaned down and looked under the car. "Good to see you, too, Uncle Kenny," she said, and she trailed after Tam across the road.

"It makes me so mad when they tell me to do what I always do," Tam complained.

"I know," Lacey said, though she knew only from friends and from television. She was lucky, she guessed. Campbell had never ordered her around like a little servant.

They entered the store and Grandpop looked up from behind the counter. "Well, look who's come," he said. "My two older granddaughters together. Eva!" He called out to Grandmom. "You go on in and take up your dad's dinner," he said to Tam.

Lacey watched Tam walk through a door at the back of the store and she wondered how Tam felt. She knew where her own stubbornness came from. If Campbell was here she would snap, "He's got two good legs. Tell him to come over here and get it." She held up the book to show Grandpop.

76

"I'm learning wildflowers," she said.

"Yup. Tam tells us you are." He looked at the book, nodding. Was this ridgewire, Lacey wondered, or only family-wire? She supposed that she, Campbell, and David were often discussed around here. "You and your grand-mom," Grandpop said, and Lacey smiled, to have him make the connection.

"Well, Lacey," Grandmom said, coming through the door with Tam behind her, carrying a plate piled with food. Tina followed Tam with a huge glass of iced tea and Teresa came behind Tina with a napkin and two fat biscuits. "Come give your grandmom a hug."

But Grandmom was the one who came, as though lead-ing a parade. When she stopped to hug Lacey, the rest of the parade marched on. Odors of food curled into her nostrils as she curled her arms around Grandmom to return the hug. There'd been no hugging since the exuberant hugging the first day they'd come, and Lacey felt awkward.

"I'm learning wildflowers," she said, showing Grand-mom the book.

"Oh, I know, and I can't tell you how happy that makes me," Grandmom said. "Come, let me show you what I have." Grandmom took hold of her hand in exactly the same way Tam did.

Lacey glanced an "excuse me" at Grandpop and followed Grandmom back through the door. She knew from Camp-bell that the house was attached to the store, but actually going through the door was like entering a foreign country. It was a house, just a house, but it was her grandmother's house. Three months ago, she would have thought she'd be completely familiar with this house by now. But this was a start.

The house backed up to the store and Grandmom walked through the kitchen to the living room. To one side was a quilting frame. Though Lacey had paid scant attention, Grandmom and Marlene made quilting talk on Sundays.

"I have a wildflower garden," Grandmom said, and walked onto the porch. Somehow Lacey hadn't thought of the house as having a front. She stood on the porch staring out at lawn, fruit trees, and a valley that swooped to the next mountain ridge. And there was Grandpop's barn.

Grandmom was already off the porch and moving to one side of the yard, where a brook twinkled and the ridge began. Lacey followed and saw coreopsis, bluets, pipsissewa, rattlesnake plantain, and fern. Grandmom pointed to some plants with two large, tonguelike leaves growing not from any stalk, but right from the ground. "Lady's slippers. I have loads of lady's slippers."

"Ohhhh," Lacey said with admiration. They weren't blooming, but she remembered the picture of the pink bulblike blossoms from her book.

Grandmom filled Lacey's head with more wildflower words than she could ever remember, then strolled back to the porch and sat on the edge. "Sit, sit," she said, patting the space beside her. "There's something I've been wanting to ask you."

Tam came through the door just then and plopped down

78

with them. Lacey was glad for the interruption. There had
been a hint of seriousness in Grandmom's invitation to sit.
Tam's smile filled the air between them. She's happy to
have her cousin and her grandmother here together, Lacey
thought.

"Tam, dear," Grandmom said. "Would you scoot along
for a bit? Lacey and I are going to talk."

Tam tilted her head and her yellow hair slid over one
shoulder. "I won't be in the way," she said.

"Well, yes, I know, dear, but Lacey and I haven't really
had *any* time together." Grandmom's smile was sugar-
coated steel and there was iron in her eyes.

The shine faded from Tam's face, her eyes. Lacey felt
the pain and thought, I'm next. Tam kept the space closed
between her head and her shoulder. "Okay, then," she
said. "Okay."

Lacey and Grandmom both watched the door where
Tam had gone. Lacey wished she had the courage to stand
up and say, "Okay, then," and walk off. Grandmom seemed
to be looking, listening, as if to be sure Tam had really
gone and was not lurking there behind the door.

Finally she said, "Lacey, there is something I wonder
about."

Lacey waited.

"I wonder what you think, how you feel about the
way your mother is living. The way she's making you
live."

"I don't know what you mean," Lacey said quickly,

knowing exactly what Grandmom meant. Why, after everything Campbell had told her about Grandmom, had she thought Grandmom would bypass this subject?

"I mean, well, the living arrangements must make you feel awkward, at least."

Lacey stared off at the wildflower garden. They hadn't talked about the fern. How could she say what she wanted to say, what she really felt? Could she tell Grandmom she was awkward only when people said things that were none of their business? Could she say that Campbell and David expressed their love for one another, which was more than Grandmom and Grandpop did, or Kenny and Marlene, or almost all the married people she knew? The words wouldn't come out. She wasn't sure she wanted them out. She wasn't sure she wanted to share this much of herself with Grandmom.

"Do you water the ferns a lot?" she asked. "Don't they need moisture?"

Grandmom spoke very slowly. "Yes. I do water them a lot. But you haven't answered me yet. I want to know how you feel, Lacey Ann."

How I feel, Lacey thought, is that all the way from Colorado I was looking forward to having a grandmother to love. A grandmother to love me. She hoped she wouldn't cry. She was not a crying sort of girl. She wished the addition of "Ann" to her name felt like love, but it didn't.

She mimicked Tam's movements of a few minutes ago and tilted her head. Her thick hair fell over her shoulder in a chunk. It didn't drip, like Tam's. "The one I feel awkward with is you," she said. She stood. "And I think I have to go now."

She went around the outside of the house and store to avoid Tam and Grandpop. She expected Grandmom to protest, to say something, to follow. Grandmom didn't speak. Or follow.

Fences

A FEW DAYS LATER AT THE BARN, AS CASUALLY AS though it were an everyday occurrence, David said, "I have bought the barn and seven acres."

Lacey's mouth flew open.

"Heyyy," David said, reaching for her ankle. "Grab her quick before she flies away."

Holding her breath, Lacey listened to what she already knew he would say next.

"We will clear the pasture, build a fence, and get a horse. Do you think you can handle it, Old Lace?" he asked.

"David, David, David," she said, and hugged him as fiercely as Grandmom had hugged her that first day.

"Equal partners?" he asked, shaking her hand.

"Equal partners," she said.

Since he was teaching workshops all day, every day but Sunday, pasture clearing and fence building were evenings-until-dark jobs. Days, Lacey crisscrossed the two acres that would soon be pasture and transplanted black-eyed Susans, creeping lespedeza and, of course, trillium. "Tam, Tam, come help me plant a wildflower garden," she said to Tam. But Tam was too busy to come. She wondered if the idea would spark Grandmom to come help, but Grandmom didn't come, either.

Soon the ground would be turned by a borrowed tractor, then tromped and grazed by a horse. A horse, a horse! The word galloped through Lacey's head day and night. What kind? What color? She'd like a red one, a sorrel, and she'd name it Starfire.

Harris, the man Tam said Uncle Kenny called a wimp, came to help set fence posts. They used locust wood that was so hard and rot-resistant, Harris said, the posts would last for fifty years. "Then you pull them up and put the other end down for another fifty."

The men used a strange-looking gadget called a "come along" to stretch the fence wire taut. Between the pasture and the barn they set posts for a paddock that would have a board fence and three gates—one to the wide doorway of the barn, the second to the pasture, and a third to the driveway. Harris came to work on the paddock fence while David was at the Craft School. Lacey, who wanted to see every posthole dug, every post set, every section of fence stretched, every board nailed, hung around him watching.

"Want to help?" Harris asked.

"Yes," she said. "I'm a good board holder."

"I mean for you to hammer," he said. "David says you wield a fine hammer."

"Yes," she said, "for making nails, not for hammering them."

"It's not that different," he said. "Just like in blacksmithing, the angle and accuracy of the hammer blow are essential."

For breaks, they wandered down to the creek where the water cooled the air and the arms of the trees held the cool air down. Out in the open, though, the air was sultry. Lacey and Harris pulled at their short sleeves and bent their heads to the cloth to wipe sweaty foreheads. Her thick hair was clipped on the sides and pulled back into a ponytail and his was in a single braid.

"I'll bet you don't have a rubber band on you," he said, wiping his beard, then braiding it. Lacey thought of the first night she'd seen him, when she'd thought he could put his beard in a ponytail, but she had never thought of him braiding it.

"I have a hair clip," she said, offering one of her pink clasps as a joke. She unfastened one, and tendrils of hair fell toward her forehead.

"What about your hair?" he asked.

"One will hold it," she said, freeing the other clip and pulling the strands to the top of her head to secure them.

Looking as solemn as Scrooge, Harris fastened the pink

84

clip to the end of his braided beard. Lacey put a hand to her mouth, not knowing whether or not to laugh, then Harris grinned and winked, and they resumed working on the paddock fence.

Lacey kept asking Tam to come over and Tam kept insisting on meeting at Flat Rock.

"I can't," Lacey said. "The sooner we have everything ready, the sooner we can get the horse." They'd already started horse shopping and, to add to the excitement, they were looking for a mare in foal.

"You don't work all day every day, do you?" Tam asked. The words echoed Lacey's own of a month ago.

"I do," she said, feeling guilty to be so busy. Was it possible, she wondered, that there really hadn't been enough to do a few weeks ago? She and Harris were building a stall just inside the barn door, with a blind side to the forge so the horse wouldn't be frightened by the fire. David had cut an extra door outside the paddock area so they could enter the barn without going through the paddock. He'd made signs to go above both doors. One read PEOPLE, and the other read PEOPLE WITH HORSES.

"You can ride," Lacey promised, thinking it the finest offer in the world.

"I don't want to ride no old horse," Tam said.

"We can have a picnic by the creek," Lacey said.

"It won't be the same," Tam said. "It's not our special place. It's not Flat Rock."

"There are lots of special places," Lacey said. "And it's the same creek. Our creek. Bitter Creek."

"It's the opposite way," Tam said, as though that should make a difference. "What are you doing that's so important? I know you're not stretching fence, because that's too hard."

Lacey felt a fence between them as real as the one going up around the pasture. "I'm helping with a board fence around the paddock," she said. "I'm helping build the stall. And I'm transplanting some of the wildflowers from out of the pasture."

There was a long pause. Then Tam said, "You and Grandmom and them old flowers," and she hung up.

So Lacey agreed to another Flat Rock day, this time walking from the barn to meet Tam at Bitter Creek. She kept turning, looking back, wishing Flat Rock was on the part of the creek that ran below the barn. It was Flat Rock, not the barn, that was the opposite way.

Tam was waiting, sitting on the board sidewalk in front of the house and garage. "I got us a cold drink," she said, holding out a can of orange soda to Lacey. The two of them walked along sucking citrus from the holes in the pop-top cans.

"What're you looking for?" Tam asked, and Lacey realized she was still turning back, still regretting every step that took her farther from the barn.

"Oh. Cars," she said. "This road is so narrow." Rocks and rhododendron loomed above them on the one side and fell away to the creek on the other.

"Hot, too," Tam said, leaving the asphalt for the grassy edges.

"Why don't you wear shoes?" Lacey asked.

"In summer?" Tam asked, as though Lacey's question was crazy.

By now they knew the exact break in the foliage to leave the road for the flat rock. Moving their arms like swimmers, they slipped through a grove of shoulder-high poplar seedlings. Enormous tulip-shaped leaves reached for the sun.

On the rock, Tam stretched out just like always, as though she were a seedling reaching for the sun. Lacey scooped a handful of pebbles from a crevice and pitched them one by one toward the water.

Tam mistook the restlessness. "I guess you don't need a cousin for a friend now that you and Grandmom are friends," she said.

Lacey's arm stopped mid-throw, her fingers not parting to release the pebble. "What?" she said. "What?"

"Private talks on the porch and all," Tam said.

A grunt of air rose in her, a "ha" that was not a laugh. She remembered that day, her own awkwardness, the hurt on Tam's face.

"I've had talks like that with Grandmom all my life," Tam said. "I've learned how to cook and to quilt and to tend the store. Even pump gas."

Big deal, Lacey thought. Flip a lever and poke a nozzle in the gas tank, pull a trigger and listen for the slurp sounds that let you know the tank is full. Most nozzles clicked off automatically, anyway. She knew how to pump gas. She also knew there was something fragile here in this conversation. "I'm learning wildflowers," she said.

"That's just one thing," Tam said. "Wildflowers." She nearly spat the word as though wildflowers were some awful thing. "I been knowing Grandmom all my life. You could, too, if Campbell hadn't taken you off like that."

"I told you about that," Lacey said, and she jerked off her sneakers and climbed down the rock. Here in hot summer, with water only to her shins, her eyeballs went cold from the chill of the water.

"Yeah, and I don't believe it!" Tam shouted, her words crashing down with the water.

What was she doing barefoot in Bitter Creek, Lacey wondered, when she wanted to be home preparing barn and pasture for the horse? Still, she moved even farther, wading to the other side. Tall, stalky plants with white and pink walnut-sized buds bordered the creek here. Was it turtlehead or snakehead? Without consulting her book, she didn't know which, and she hadn't even brought it this time. She snapped one off to carry back. In the chill of the water, with the tender blossom in her hand, she realized Tam felt in danger of losing Grandmom to her. Another unlaughing "ha" rose up.

"Nothing has anything to do with Grandmom," Lacey said when she'd recrossed the creek. Words. To try to make them both feel better. "The reason I didn't want to come is because there's so much work to be done to get ready for the horse." As water dripped down her legs, she moved her feet to make dark, barefoot designs on Flat Rock, a foot-flower, with her heel as center.

88

"Well, let's go, then," Tam snapped, and was up and moving before the flower was finished.

Lacey felt slapped, trying to make an understanding and not having it understood. Almost anyone would understand the excitement about a horse. Anyone but Tam.

"Okay. Let's," she said, and scrambled up the bank, back through the poplar grove.

Tam literally hotfooted it down the road, choosing the sting of the pavement over the soft coolness of grass.

"Ta-a-am," Lacey said finally. She was taller, had longer legs, but was hopping and skipping to keep up. She wanted to say she was sorry, but her feelings were confused. She wasn't sorry she was geting a horse, wasn't sorry to be able to help get ready for it. She wanted to say she didn't want them to be angry and that Grandmom had nothing to do with it, but somehow Grandmom did.

When they came around the curve and saw the stores, there was David's truck in front of Kenny's. Good, Lacey thought. Home that much faster. And she smiled at herself for thinking of the barn, the land, as "home."

Kenny was just slamming the hood of the truck. "You girls didn't stay long," he said.

Lacey shrugged. "Where's David?" Kenny pointed a wrench across toward the Gas and Gro. Lacey looked at the storefront, willing David to come *now*.

"Daddy, will you tell Lacey it isn't true that Grandmom tried to take her away from Aunt Campbell?" Tam flashed a now-you'll-find-out look at Lacey and planted a fist on her hip.

An old red bandanna was hanging like a signal flag from Kenny's back pocket. He took it and wiped his face, his hands, the wrench.

"Well?" Tam said.

"I can't tell you that, baby," Kenny said. "Because it's true."

"But Grandmom says—" Tam started.

"Never mind what your grandmom says," Kenny said. "There were lawyers, and warrants, and that's all the more I'm going to say about it. It's gone on long enough, now."

Lacey had no sense of triumph, though she could see Tam felt defeated. It had gone on long enough, that part was also true. But the word "warrant" snaked out and looped around her as though it might even yet take hold of her and drag her away from Campbell. A chill went through her as surely as though she still had her feet in Bitter Creek.

"Well," Tam said, "well." Her mouth wrinkled and tightened on the small face. "If Grandmom did that, your mother must have been some terrible kind of mother!" On the huff of words, Tam puffed off across the road, ignoring Kenny's calling of her name. David emerged from the red door, smiled, and spoke to Tam, then shrugged and looked after her as she went in.

"It's not true," Kenny said to Lacey, as she watched David come toward them. "Campbell was a good mother. Campbell was always a good mother."

"It's you," David said, curling an arm around Lacey. "You staying or coming with me?"

"Coming," she said, and she climbed onto the truck seat, not able to look at Tam's last track or back at Kenny, either.

"What was that all about?" David asked when they had road under them and Bitter Creek behind.

"Nothing," Lacey said, wondering how "nothing" could get so huge.

In the night the incessant drone of katydids began.

"When do they stop?" Lacey asked.

"First frost," Campbell said.

"I mean tonight. When do they stop tonight?"

"Dawn. You might as well get used to it. I like them, myself. Sounds like a symphony."

"Sounds like noise to me," Lacey said.

"Listen to the rhythm. It's as though they have a conductor out there in the woods."

"Yeah," Lacey said. "David with a fork."

A few days later David asked, "What's the matter, Old Lace? Tam?"

Lacey shrugged. They were eating supper by the creek and Campbell had taken off her shoes and was trailing her toes in the water. She hadn't told them what Tam had said about Campbell. Lacey knew Tam had said it because she was upset, but that didn't make it feel any better. It seemed so ridiculous that Tam could be, well, jealous because she'd learned some wildflowers.

"I tell you what," David said. "I'll get in touch with everyone and tell them dinner is here next Sunday."

Lacey's and Campbell's words hit the air at the same time.

Lacey said "Oh, David, really?" while Campbell said, "No." She pulled her feet from the water and clutched her knees. Campbell's "no" made Lacey think, maybe, no.

"You won't have to do a thing," David said. "I'll fix everything and do the dishes, too."

"I don't want them here," Campbell said. "Them" did not mean Kenny or Marlene, Tam, Tina, or Teresa, Lacey knew, and probably not even Grandpop. "Them" meant only Grandmom, who had zipped up the driveway of the old Ford place so often at first, but had set neither tire nor foot here on this road in the months since they'd rented the barn. Only to Lacey did "them" include Tam, too.

"Well, I hate to be autocratic," David said. "You know I consider this *our* place, but that means it's mine, too, and I'd like to have the family over for dinner."

"I won't come," Campbell said, still staring at her toes.

Was anything the same, Lacey wondered, except for these Sunday dinners when Grandmom called Campbell every kind of soup there was? They'd been having them on the western-style sidewalk in front of Kenny's the past few times and it had been fun. It would be fun to have it at the barn. She sucked in her breath. "I'll help," she said.

Later, on the way back to the house, David pulled up in front of Kenny's. Lacey and Campbell stayed in the cab of the pickup and Lacey watched David open the door of the house and stick his head and shoulders in.

"Kenny? Marlene? Dinner at the barn this Sunday." His voice was muffled and his position in the doorway reminded Lacey of half a salamander, but the whole David reappeared.

"Hey, that's a deal," Lacey heard Kenny reply, and David crossed the street to call the same message into the Gas and Gro.

Lacey peeled and cut potatoes until she thought they could feed thirty, not just ten. She mounded and flattened cold, ground beef for hamburgers until her hands were nearly frostbitten. David finished the potato salad, cooked a huge panful of green beans, and baked a sour-cream cake. Campbell single-mindedly stayed on the side porch, tooling oak leaves and acorns onto the skirt of a leather saddle. When Lacey and David loaded the food into the truck, Campbell was still determinedly lost in the oak forest.

"You coming?" David asked once. When there was no answer, he said, "It's your choice."

Kenny and Marlene and the girls were there right at twelve. Kenny's hands reached out to touch, to hold the tools of David's trade. Marlene was impressed with the wildflower garden and all the things Lacey had transplanted. Tina and Teresa were excited about the prospective horse.

"We don't have anything but an old cow," Tina said.

"Uh-uh," Teresa said, blond hair clinging to her cheeks as she nodded and said, "Chickens."

If these four Bittners needed melting, it was done, but Tam wandered around like a glacier.

About twelve-thirty, they looked up to the crunch of tires on gravel. It was not Grandmom's blue-gray Buick, but Grandpop's silver pickup with only Grandpop inside. Shaking his head, he descended from the truck and walked toward them. "I tried to tell Eva—" he began, but David stopped him.

"Campbell's not here, either, but let's not talk about it right now, okay?"

Grandpop nodded.

"And let's for godsakes eat!" Kenny said.

Polly

THE HORSE WAS A SORREL. RED ALL OVER. RED MANE, tail, ankles, all. No white blaze or white socks.

"Starfire," Lacey said immediately, but the horse already had a name. Pretty Polly. "Pretty Polly?" Lacey said, wrinkling her nose in disgust. "Sounds like a parrot." At the sound of her name, Polly wrinkled her nose and snickered. "Can't even call her by her initials," Lacey said, reaching out and touching the velvet softness of the muzzle, and she knew she would not try to change the horse's name. A foal was due in the spring and that would be her Starfire.

In the truck, she knelt on the seat and looked backwards, watching Polly strain for footing as David crept around

95

curves. Her legs could already feel the bow of straddling a horse again.

At the barn, they led Polly down the trailer ramp and across the paddock. "For sweet feed and sweet talk," Campbell said.

Lacey scooped a bucket into the sack of honey-coated grain. Above her, the loft was already fat with hay. All three of them patted, stroked, and said affectionate words as Polly nuzzled into the bucket and munched grain.

"That's music to my ears," Lacey said as Polly crunched.

When Campbell saddled Polly with the one she had just finished tooling, David said, "Campbell, that saddle's for Colorado. We can't afford a handmade saddle." He had borrowed a saddle for them to use on Polly, although Campbell had made this acorn and oak-leaf saddle for a sixteen hands' quarterhorse, just Polly's size.

Campbell rubbed Polly with one hand and the saddle with the other. "Polly's our first, very own horse. She deserves the best."

"Yeah," said Lacey.

"Campbell, don't use this horse as an excuse," David said sharply, and he began uncinching the saddle.

Lacey and Campbell looked up in surprise.

"What?" Campbell said.

"You've let spring and summer go by without taking your work to any of the craft fairs," he said. He slid the saddle off the horse and flopped it across the paddock fence. "You didn't put this saddle on Polly because you wanted Polly to have the best." He picked up the borrowed saddle and set it on Polly's back. "You're afraid to send it to Mr. Whosis in Colorado for big bucks."

He fastened the borrowed saddle onto Polly and patted her flank. "You're scared that if you prove you can take care of yourself, you might have to do it."

Glaring at David, brown eyes to brown eyes, Campbell unfastened the borrowed saddle and flopped it over the paddock fence. Then she hoisted the acorn and oak-leaf saddle and recinched it on Pretty Polly.

David stalked off, his booted feet springing puffs of dust from the dry ground.

Campbell motioned to Lacey, and Lacey stuck her foot into the left stirrup and swung herself up and onto the saddle, patting and talking horse-talk all the while. She was the first to sit on Polly, the first to sit in this saddle. "Let me lead her," Campbell said, and Lacey leaned and patted as Campbell led them around the paddock.

"Polly's a tall horse," Lacey said, paying relentless attention to the horse and ignoring what had gone on between the people. Her favorite in Colorado had been Misty, a black, thirteen hands' quarterhorse and Welsh-pony mix.

"Big for a quarterhorse," Campbell said, handing Lacey the reins. Lacey walked Polly around the paddock on her own. Home, she'd often thought, was Campbell and David. But today home was the back of a horse. She was ready for a tall horse.

Kenny and Marlene brought Tina and Teresa to see the horse. Kenny rode. Marlene wouldn't. Lacey led the girls around the paddock.

"End of the month, let's have dinner here again," David said.

Teresa said, "Oh, boy!"

Campbell gave the I-won't-come look.

Kenny said, "I don't know why you want to do that if it's going to make people feel excluded." Lacey wondered if he was talking about Tam as well as Campbell and Grandmom. She had thought sure Tam would come to see the horse.

"Wait a minute," David said. "I am including everyone. Anyone who doesn't come is excluding herself." He looked at Campbell.

Grandpop came to see the horse, mounted Polly, and galloped around the pasture.

"I didn't know you could ride," Lacey said when he returned to the paddock.

"Where do you think she learned about horses?" he said, tilting his head toward Campbell. "Thomas Elihu Bittner was one of the first men to come into these parts. Came over the mountains on horseback. All the Bittners know how to ride."

Lacey looked at Campbell. She hadn't known this, she'd thought Campbell learned about horses in Colorado. A current of tenderness flowed between Grandpop and Campbell and drifted onto Lacey. She was a Bittner, and she knew how to ride.

"Why don't you have a horse now?" Lacey asked, scarcely able to believe he didn't. Campbell had said they had a barn.

98

Grandpop stroked Polly's side. "Oh, well. Between fishing and the store, there doesn't seem to be time for a horse."

Horses would be her fishing, Lacey decided. Horses would be her store. She would always have time for a horse.

"Tom, you're welcome to keep a horse here for the cost of the feed," David said. "We'll do the daily care and you just come saddle up whenever you want."

Lacey could tell by his eyes and his grin that if Grandpop hadn't been melted before, he was now.

"Dinner at the barn again the last Sunday of August," David said.

Grandpop nodded. "Fine. Fine. Sounds fine to me."

Lacey thought Campbell might object to David's offer of keeping a horse for Grandpop. The horses were really Campbell's business. Perhaps Campbell was saving her protest. Or perhaps, Lacey thought, Campbell was melting, too.

Campbell moved her leatherwork to the barn and wrote a letter of delay to Mr. Whosis in Colorado and began another saddle. "Three hundred hours' work on a saddle like that," Campbell said. Lacey was amazed, when she followed Campbell's arithmetic, that three hundred hours was less than eight weeks of forty-hour workweeks. Three hundred hours seemed an eternity, as long as fifty years.

Every minute in the barn was Lacey's own eternity. The rough wood of gates, the toughness of hooves, the coarse hair on mane and tail were all pearls to Lacey's hands. The earth, hay, and hot horse smells were like extra oxygen to her nose and lungs. She never even minded trundling the manure upridge to the compost heap. The muffled thumps of Polly moving in the stall, the snickers and whinnies, and especially the rhythmic thud of hooves as they galloped across the pasture, were sounds she hoped she would always have in her ears.

Still, and in spite of Tam's words about Campbell, she missed Tam. Now that Polly was settled, she could spare some time away. She could meet Tam at Flat Rock and walk on to the barn later. At the next Sunday dinner, she proposed it.

Tam looked as though Lacey had suggested a trip to hell. "Flag corps practice starts tomorrow," Tam said.

"In the middle of summer?"

"School starts in two weeks," Tam said. "Summer is almost over."

School? The word hit Lacey like a smack. School? She was just getting started on her summer. And after all the begging in the spring, she noticed that Tam did not, now, ask her to join flag corps.

As she rode round and round the pasture, she thought and thought about Tam. How fast June and July had passed, those Flat Rock days. Wasn't it possible, she wondered, to have a horse and a cousin, too?

At supper one night, she asked, "What would you think about me joining flag corps?" In the spring, Cheryl had said maybe Lacey would decide to join later.

David and Campbell looked at one another. "Fine," said Campbell.

"I mean, it's every day and someone will have to take me and pick me up."

"Fine," said David.

"I'll have to call Cheryl and see if it's all right," she said. She had found that Cheryl was "Shirl" in spite of herself.

"Hey, yeah, great," Cheryl said, and the next morning at nine o'clock, Lacey held a blue and gold flag in her hands.

"You just want to get in on everything, don't you?" Tam said, looking at Lacey with surprise but no delight. Just when Lacey was supposed to show some spirit, it seemed to drain out through a hole in her big toe. She'd only come to make amends with Tam, but Tam was not amending. Now flag corps, it seemed, was added to wildflowers and horses on Tam's list of irritations with Lacey. But Cheryl's mother directed them in some routines and soon Lacey was absorbed in marching rhythms and floating flags, the snap of heels and of the gold and blue. Her favorite move was when they swung the flags to left or right, not at the same time, but immediately following the one before. It was like waves of flags, an ocean of flags.

Afterwards, Campbell was waiting right on time. So was Grandmom.

"I could bring her, you know," Grandmom told Campbell. "I could take you back and forth," she said to Lacey. Tam climbed into the Buick without even saying goodbye.

"Maybe I could ride with them," Lacey said, as Campbell followed the Buick down the road. Trapped together in the car, Tam was bound to talk. But Campbell was not enthusiastic.

"Maybe you could," David said later. "If we can't melt them, maybe we should let them melt us. What do you think, Lace? Come with me now. I think it's time to start buying gas at Bittner's. Come on, Minestrone, you come, too."

"Don't you dare call me that," Campbell said, cutting off the laugh that was on the way up through Lacey's throat. Campbell busied herself with the dishes as an excuse.

Tam ran out to pump the gas, but when she saw who it was, she looked like she wanted to run right back in again. As unamused as Campbell, she removed the gas cap and inserted the nozzle. Lacey caught her bottom lip in her teeth because, for the first time, she saw the Bittner in Tam. Rather, the Campbell. That look could have been traced directly from the faces of Campbell and Grandmom.

David went into the store and left Tam with the truck. Lacey leaned out the window and spoke to Tam. "He's going to see if Grandmom will take me back and forth to flag corps practice. Do you mind?"

"Why should I mind?" Tam said, tossing her head, flinging the words over the top of the truck.

"I thought you might even be glad," Lacey ventured.

"Why should I be glad?" Tam said to the sky. She removed the nozzle and returned it to the pump, replaced the gas cap, and trotted off to the store.

The next day, Grandmom crunched up the driveway and tooted the horn for Lacey, even though Lacey was standing right there, ready. Tam squiggled over so close to Grandmom that Grandmom said, "Well, you don't have to squash me, Tam, there's plenty of room."

At practice, Lacey tried to keep from tripping over her feet as they practiced maneuvers. Left face march, where the entire line turned at once, and left column march, where you didn't turn until you reached the point where the first person in the line had turned, confused her. She found herself going straight when everyone left-faced, and turning left when they were continuing a column. And twice she moved her flag so totally wrong, it almost became a lance.

"You should have been to spring practice," Tam said afterwards. "Then you'd know." Tam climbed into the back seat.

Without anyone to get ahead of or stay behind, Grandmom drove at a normal speed. As they passed the road to the barn, Lacey looked up with pleasure, knowing she and Campbell would be back here soon. At Bitter Creek, Grandmom pulled up in front of the Gas and Gro. Tam scrambled out the back door and Grandmom turned off the ignition and got out as well.

"Come on in for a minute," Grandmom said.

Lacey wasn't inclined to move. She started to say, I'm supposed to go on home, but she remembered what David had said about letting "them melt us." Reluctantly, she opened the passenger door and slid out. What could be more natural, she told herself. I'm just stopping by my grandmother's store for a minute.

"Good to see you, Lacey," said Grandpop, from where he sat perched on a stool behind the counter. When he looked at her, his eyes twinkled. She'd never noticed that before. "How's our Pretty Polly?" Lacey relaxed and started talking about how much hay Polly ate, how much grain, and how the pasture grass was growing. She didn't even notice Tam and Grandmom had gone, or where, but suddenly she realized a minute was up. Lots of minutes. How many? Just as she was trying to see Grandpop's watch, without asking the time, Grandmom came back into the store from the back door.

"Oh, I wondered where you were," Lacey said.

"Did you think I'd got lost?" Grandmom said. "Or did you think you were lost?" Tam was in the doorway behind her.

"It's just that I have to get home."

"This is your home," Grandmom said. Was Grandmom going to try to keep her? "Anywhere around here is your home. And what's your all-fired hurry? We're going to have lunch first. I never thought I'd have you back in Bitter Creek and never see you."

"I, uh, have to go," Lacey said, edging backwards toward the door. She had heard about divorced parents who kidnapped the children from one another. What about grandparents? Her feelings were so mixed up.

"I'll carry you home after lunch," Grandmom said.

"I, uh, have to go now," Lacey said. "I have to be home for lunch. I'll walk, thank you." She nodded and backed and almost bowed, but no matter how hard she swallowed, the lump in her throat would not go down. They didn't call for her to come back, didn't run after her with offers to take her home now. All the way home, she looked back, first thinking they would come and she would refuse the ride, then thinking they might zoom around a curve and pop her off the road to lie there, broken in the rocks and scrub like an old doll. She snorted hot breath to evaporate the tears that kept gathering in her throat. When she got home, she would cry and cry and cry like Campbell had when Tony left, and Ralph, but she would not have them find her crying on the road.

"Where have you been?" Campbell said, fear and anger making her pounce. "I wanted to come find you, but I didn't want to leave in case you phoned." When Lacey told what had happened, Campbell was furious. "Well, that's the end of that little experiment."

When David heard, he thought otherwise. "You did well, Old Lace," he said, amused and proud. "She tried to boss you and intimidate you and you refused to be bossed and intimidated. What's more, you were even polite about it. You kept your integrity."

Lacey felt herself go all hot. "What about her integrity?"

He cocked his head briefly and lifted one shoulder. "That's one of life's hardest lessons, Lace. There's not a fripping thing you can do about anyone else's integrity. If you can manage to keep your own, that's quite a lot."

"Well, I'll keep my integrity out of her car from now on," she said.

"I think you ought to keep riding with her, Lacey.

If she shows up to take you," David said.

"Do you want me to be kidnapped, is that what?" Lacey asked. The threats of ten years ago still seemed to be hanging over her.

"Now wait a minute," he said. Lacey and Campbell had cooked and David was dealing plates, knives, forks, napkins around the table. Campbell spooned macaroni-and-cheese into one serving dish and green peas into another. A bed of raw spinach covered with sliced eggs, tomatoes, and cucumbers nested in a wooden salad bowl. "You have her half-melted already."

"Huh!" Lacey said, her explosive breath matching the crack of ice cubes as she plunked them into glasses. If the Antarctic was half-melted, the part still frozen would be Grandmom, she thought.

"What's the worst possible thing that could happen?" he asked, as they all sat down. He flourished his fork as though his points would be more persuasive if slung off the tines. "Suppose she picks you up in the morning and drives off into the country and kills you?"

"David!" Campbell said.

"Well, it's the worst thing I could think of," he said.

"Say she just drives off into the country and we don't ever see either of them again."

"I'd get away," Lacey said.

"So, then, what's the worst possible thing that could happen if Lacey rides back and forth with Grandmom?" He waggled the fork, stirring air, as though conducting their responses.

"She could not bring me home," Lacey said. "She could stop at the store, like today, and I'd have to walk." Odd, how unscary that seemed now.

"What if she locked you in a closet?"

"You'd come find me," Lacey said.

"Ri-i-ight!" he said, jabbing the fork as for the finale. "I'd come storming into the store, into the house, looking in the freezer, under beds, flinging open closet doors. You bet I would."

"Oh, David," Campbell said.

"Look," he said, "even if we never have a good relationship with them, or if we have no relationship with them at all, I don't want it to be because we haven't made every possible effort or because any of us have buckled to intimidation." He speared some macaroni, slid it into his mouth, and shook the fork at Campbell. "You talk like you're so independent, Campbell, but you're not. Your one independent act was to take the baby and run."

"I had to," Campbell said.

"I know you had to," he said. "There was only one way for you to get away, and you did it."

"I certainly did."

"But I want it to be different for Lacey. I don't want her to have to give ground to keep from giving up."

They hashed it out until every green pea was eaten, until there was no macaroni or spinach salad for David to scrape into the garbage or put away in the refrigerator. It was as though the discussion took extra energy and they needed every bite for fuel. The conclusion was that she would ride with Grandmom if, indeed, Grandmom showed up.

"Should we call her?" Lacey asked.

"Oh, no, let's just see," David said.

Lacey shook her head. "I don't think she'll come."

"I'm betting she will," he said, and he set one of his hands palm down on the table and nodded to Lacey. She set one of her hands on top of his. "She thinks she has the upper hand," he said, and he slowly put his other hand on top of Lacey's. "But she'll see she doesn't." Lacey grinned and topped his hand with her other one. Then he pulled his bottom hand out and put it on top and she did the same until their hands were flying, bottom to top.

"You two," Campbell said.

To Lacey's astonishment, the Buick turned into the driveway in the morning. David suggested that Lacey be standing there, ready, and she was. Nonetheless, Grandmom blew the horn.

When Tam opened the door, Lacey reached around and pulled up the rear latch. "You don't have to scoot over," she said. "I'll get in back." This had been her own idea.

Grandmom started right in telling about Teresa losing another tooth, but Lacey noticed that the chatter was filled with nervous energy. The energy seemed to bounce around the car. Grandmom, Lacey realized, had been surprised to see her. Grandmom had been ready for battle and the fact that there was no battle had released energy that now had nowhere to go. Somehow the balance of power had shifted. As they zipped along through Bitter Creek, toward Savory,

Lacey was both giddy and frightened. She didn't want power over Grandmom.

During marching practice, the power sank to her feet and her feet made no wrong moves, and she knew. Who she had power over was herself.

Cheryl's mother said, "Look at Lacey. How quickly she catches on."

The Cabin

AFTER PRACTICE FOR THE NEXT THREE DAYS, GRAND-
mom stopped by the store. Right after, David "happened"
along to take Lacey home or to the barn. Then Grandmom
started taking Lacey home or dropping her off at the gravel
road, whichever Lacey said.

Conversation in the car during the trips to Savory was
not really conversation at all. If Lacey said something about
Polly, Tam talked about flag corps. When Lacey joined in
about flag corps, Tam said something about a square on
Grandmom's quilt. When Lacey commented on the quilt,
Tam rattled off about the gas pump getting stuck.

"I hate the way everyone talks here," Lacey said to David.

He nodded. "You mean you hate the way Tam won't talk?"

"Well, her, too," Lacey said, ignoring his implication. "The way she says 'hit' and 'hissef' and 'skwar.' " They were having sandwiches on the creek bank and she piled two mayonnaised slices of bread with tomato, pickles, onion, and alfalfa sprouts.

"Well, Lacey, don't you lak to wash your har when hit gets dirty?" Campbell asked.

Her hands already occupied with a sandwich, Lacey did her best to cover her ears with her shoulders. "Oh, stop!" she said.

"That's my native language you're talking about," Campbell said.

"You don't say 'hit,' " Lacey said.

"That's because I lost my accent."

"Like me," David said.

"But ah kin git rat back into hit," Campbell said.

"And you liked when I make speech like new days," David said. He punctuated his sentence by crunching on a stalk of celery.

"That's different," Lacey said, taking a piece of celery and duplicating his crunch. All she knew of his accent was when he lapsed into it for fun. He knew several languages and didn't consider he had mastered a language until he could speak it without an accent. She loved it when he said "aleebee" for alibi, or "loolabee" for lullaby.

"Why?" he asked. "Why is that different?"

"It just is," she said. "It's different when it's a foreign

accent than when it's people who should know better."

"Uh-oh," Campbell said. "Do I detect a little prejudice sneaking out?"

"No," Lacey said, but it was a feeble "no." She hadn't thought of it as prejudice, the way she hated hearing them talk, the way Grandmom spoke of "carrying" them to practice.

"How boring it would be if we all talked the same way," David said with a clipped British accent. "What you don't realize, Old Lace, is that being isolated back in these hills, these people have retained some of the old English speech patterns. Some of what you think is mountain-talk is actually more pure English than you speak."

"Not 'hit,' " she said.

"Especially 'hit,' " he said. "You don't really speak English at all. You speak American. And as soon as I finish eating, I'm going in thar and lat a far. Will you help me with hit? We'll get to work and celebrate the differences."

She frowned, and when enough time had passed that she thought he might let the subject go, she spoke in her very best American. "I wish we lived right here."

Immediately, David pointed. "I think it will nestle in nicely right there, without our having to cut any trees. The creek will sing to us all night."

"Wha-a-aat?" Lacey asked.

"Our cabin," he said. "Our A-frame cabin." He spiked his hands up into the sides of an A and Lacey could already envision the spires angling into the limbs of the poplar trees. She had meant, live in the barn. They had, once, in Colorado. But a cabin would be terrific.

"It will be like a treehouse," she said.

"Indeed it will," he said. "And you will help me build it. We'll have a window where we can look out and see trillium." And even though it was summer, and there was no window, they already saw next spring's trillium through the window.

"Oh, David," she said, hugging him. "It will be so perfect." Already Campbell had made a place in the barn for her leatherwork and David had a commission for an important blacksmith project. And she would be here riding Polly up mountain and down meadow through the long, languid afternoons.

One day soon after, as the road uncurled before them, Grandmom said, "Look, there's the joe-pye. It's too soon, too soon."

"What do you mean?" Lacey asked, seeing the tall, rose-colored blossoms that swayed over fencerows and fields. How could it be too soon or too late? Whenever the wildflowers bloomed was the right time, wasn't it?

"When the joe-pye blooms, autumn is on the way," Grandmom said.

"Autumn!" Lacey said. "It's the middle of August. I thought this was the South!"

Grandmom said what Campbell had said in the late spring when there was still a nip in the air. "It's the mountain south."

As though joe-pye or Grandmom had bidden it, the

sourwoods began to turn scarlet overnight. The heavy air of summer fled and a draft of autumn lightness came behind, even though no change registered on the thermometer.

School started. Adjusting to junior high was easy; Lacey was in a different building, but on the same campus, with the same classmates, including Bradley. He didn't put a mouse on her seat, but he smiled at her a lot. She smiled back. Some days he hung around and watched flag corps practice. Was he watching her, she wondered, or everyone?

David began to build the cabin. Lacey grieved over every foundation post, sill, and joist that went up without her.

"Why didn't you start it in the summer when I had time?" Lacey asked.

"Because I didn't have time, Lace bug," David said. From now on, most of his workshops would be on weekends. This gave him time for the cabin and for the commission project he was working on.

"I should never have started flag corps," she said.

"Sure you should have," Campbell said. "Are you enjoying it?"

"Yes, but—" She let her voice trail off. When she left for school soon after daylight and returned just before dark, days went by when she didn't even ride Polly. So much for always having time for horses.

The last Sunday in August she and David baked chicken-and-squash casserole and boiled corn for dinner at the barn. Campbell didn't help or come. Neither did Grandmom.

Nor did Tam. One by one, it seemed to Lacey, they were losing, not gaining.

But September was a magician. With school and homework, flag corps and Polly and cabin building, time vanished.

The flag corps, in addition to practice, was doing drills during halftime at the junior high football games on Friday afternoons. Some games were at the school field in Savory and others were in Mountain Home, or Logan, or Gordyville. Harris was helping David with the cabin, but since they were working on it weekdays, not weekends, Lacey was only inspecting the progress, not participating. Once again, David claimed a Sunday for dinner at the barn and again Lacey helped. Campbell came.

David eased Lacey's sorrow over missing out on the cabin construction by talking to her about his new project. "Do you think I can make anything as delicate as a trillium out of iron?" he asked.

She knew he could. He'd made leaves that were as slender as, well, leaves. The project was a wrought-iron railing for a posh new resort near Asheville. They wanted the railing to incorporate mountain themes and David had designed one with an outline of mountains below the top rail. Leaves and flowers would be tumbling down the mountains.

"You're the wildflower expert," he told her. "Will you help me decide which ones to use?"

"Fire pinks," she said. She knew what he would say next, so she said it first. "Equal partners?"

He grinned and shook her hand. "Equal partners," he said.

Most days, now, Grandmom was dropping her off at the end of the gravel road leading to the barn. One day toward the middle of October, when some of the leaves were the color of Bradley's hair, Grandmom said, "Lacey, won't you just once come home with me for a few minutes? I have something special I want to show you."

Since Grandmom had asked instead of commanded, an inclination to say "yes" rose up in Lacey. "Yes," she said. "But I have to stop by and tell them, first."

"It won't be for long," Grandmom said, showing no sign of slowing down.

"Well, I have to tell them," Lacey insisted. "Or I can't go. Just let me out and I'll run down and back." She envisioned a walk back from the store and regretted being so agreeable. Then Grandmom did slow down. Lacey reached for the door handle, ready to hop out, but Grandmom pulled onto the gravel and kept going, down to the creek and across the old plank bridge.

"Stop here," Lacey said, when they were near the cabin. Hammer sounds rang in her ear when she zizzed down the window. She wanted to leap from the car and go help. Instead, she called out to David. "I'm going to Grandmom's for a few minutes, okay?"

"Sure, Lacey. Okay," he called out. His eyebrows raised and he gave her a thumbs-up gesture. "See you later."

"Can I borrow a hair clip, Lacey?" Harris asked.

Lacey laughed. Grandmom backed and turned around. "What did he mean by that?" Tam asked.

"Oh, just a joke," Lacey said, sorry that when Tam finally said something to her directly she didn't want to answer it openly. Tam's opinion of Harris would not be enhanced by the story of his braiding his beard and fastening it with a pink hair clasp.

As she stepped through the door that joined the back of the store with the back of the house, she had an odd, fleeting thought. This was only the second time in six months she'd been through that door. What if she were the grandmother and her granddaughter refused to come over? She'd never thought of Grandmom's feelings before, only Campbell's and David's and her own.

Grandmom led the way to the living room and stopped by the quilting frame.

"What's that?" Lacey asked, though she knew. Her spirits sank. She was going to get a quilting lesson when she would rather be helping David at the cabin.

"My quilt," Grandmom said. "I make three or four quilts a year. Several squares a week until I have enough."

Lacey stifled a sigh and fastened her eyes on Grandmom's hands as they moved across the quilt. How to be bored, in three easy lessons, she thought.

"This one might take longer," Grandmom said. "I'm making my own design and it's more complicated to figure everything out." Lacey stood there wishing-wishing-wishing she was exploring the barn, hammering with David and Harris, or trotting up the gravel road with Polly. She almost missed it when Grandmom said, "This quilt is going to be patches of Bittner history, including a square for you. Here's Thomas Elihu Bittner coming over the mountains on his horse. Here's Kenny and the shop. And how is this for you?" She was fingering pieces to be appliquéd—a fire pink, a sorrel horse's head, and a blue and gold flag.

"Oh, Grandmom!" Lacey said, gasping with delight. What about Campbell? Does Campbell have a square, she wondered? She let the question dwindle in the warmth of the moment. Finally, after all these months, there was melting. Finally, after all these months, Lacey felt her grandmother's love.

No Forevers

ONE WEEK LATER, WHEN THE TREES WERE SCREAMING yellow-orange—purple-red and leaping from the trees, David was dead.

Harris came to tell them. Harris with his same droll mouth, but no wry jokes on his tongue.

"Well, that sure took long enough," said Campbell. She was tapping a basket-weave design on the back jockey of a saddle which, she had promised David, would go to Colorado. The two men had gone to Savory for building supplies, for the skin of the cabin—siding, windows, doors. The A-beams were up. Arrows into the sky.

"We, uh, had an accident," Harris said, rubbing his thumbs

against his fingers as though he were turning a hat brim in his hands. But there was no hat.

With no feeling of foreboding whatsoever, Lacey glanced up from where she was currying Polly and looked across the paddock toward Harris's truck.

"Yeah, I see," she said. The fender was crumpled on the driver's side. "Doesn't look too bad," she said, resuming the brushstrokes on Polly. "Where's David?"

"David is, uh," Harris said, still twirling the invisible hat, "uh, dead."

There was no mistaking the word or asking for a repetition. Campbell had taken two steps toward the barn door, to see the crumpled fender, and she stopped. Lacey continued brushing Polly as though Harris had just said the sky was blue. The air was heavy with disbelief.

"Uh, someone ran the blinker light. After we'd got the stuff. Just a freak thing. I saw them, but I was already out into the intersection just a bit. I stopped. They didn't. Hit me on my side. Just the fender." He was speaking quietly. Harris always spoke quietly. His overalls were just as loose as they were the first time Lacey had seen him. His words seemed to float like the soap bubbles she made in the kitchen, full of color, full of the whole world. Then they popped and there was nothing, nothing, only these minutes, like centuries, in the barn.

"David was leaning against the door on his side and the door popped open. He laughed and grabbed for the handle, but went sailing out, laughing. Trying to get his feet under him. Laughing. He was laughing."

120

Campbell hadn't moved since Harris had pronounced the word "dead." Lacey kept moving, making those familiar strokes along the hair of a horse. No one was laughing.

"He, uh, lost his grip on the handle. Couldn't get his feet under him. He flung head first into, uh, a fire hydrant." Harris made the smallest shrug, but it rippled down his clothing to the hem of his overalls.

People came. Patricia Lamb and others from the Craft School. Kenny and Marlene. Grandmom and Grandpop. Even Fred Palmer came. Except for Grandmom, they kept repeating the same words. "Let us know if there is anything we can do." And Grandmom kept saying, "Maybe now you'll come home where you belong." Tam said, "I'm sorry about David," but Lacey was not comforted. I'll bet, she thought bitterly.

Campbell and Lacey remained as they had been that day in the barn. Campbell cried and was unmoving, unable to do anything. Lacey didn't cry and was compelled to move. She studied harder, marched harder, rode harder, fired the forge, and made nails ferociously.

Bradley, out of sympathy, she guessed, stopped smiling at her. He didn't say anything, either, but what was there to say? Words would not bring David back. Some days she was relieved when people didn't try to make words. Other days she was angry that they weren't expressing their sorrow every minute.

Meaning to be kind, Cheryl's mother said, "You can

121

take some time off, Lacey. We can work the routine around you."

"That's all right," Lacey said.

Her teachers said, "You don't have to work so hard, Lacey. You're doing fine."

What she couldn't tell them, what she couldn't even form into coherent thoughts for herself, was that she had to work. She felt that she herself was dead, but she knew she wasn't. Only if she kept working could she perhaps keep some motion going until she was alive again. David, of all people, would want her to.

Like leaving all the wildflowers of Colorado behind without knowing their names, she now had a million questions for David, about David. When he was exactly her age, his parents had been cruelly tortured and killed in one of the savage actions of the Mideast. Somehow he had kept on living. How, she wanted to know. How, she asked him now. He never answered. She didn't even know how old he was when he came to this country, who he knew here, who he lived with. He never talked about it. He had, she knew, made his own roots. When people noticed his unusual name and asked where he was from, he always said, "Colorado," which was true, but not the answer they were seeking.

Now, when Lacey poured out her questions, Campbell said, "Oh, Lacey, please don't bother me with questions."

At school they learned the word "eviscerate" and Lacey had no trouble comprehending its meaning. All her vital parts were torn out.

Mornings, Campbell drove her to the barn so she could take care of Polly. Grandmom picked her up for school from there and dropped her back there in the afternoons. Campbell was there, had been there all day, but there was not one more weave of the basket design on the saddle, not one more buckle fastened to a belt, and Polly stamped restlessly at having had company all day without having any company.

"What do you do all day?" Lacey asked.

"Walk," Campbell said. "Sit." She began to cry again and from the midst of the crying came a third muffled word. "Cry."

On weekends as Lacey shoveled manure, curried and rode Polly, she watched Campbell. Campbell roamed the boundary of the property, the perimeter of the pasture, sat in the barn or by the creek or beneath the A-beams of the cabin. She cried as she walked, cried as she sat.

Harris came, still looking like he had a hat in hand. "I'd like to help you get the cabin done," he said.

"I can't," Campbell said. "Harris, thank you, but I can't. I don't want anything touched."

"How long are you going to keep on crying?" Lacey asked, sitting cross-legged as she joined Campbell on the cabin deck one day.

Campbell sniffled and snuffled. "I can't help it," she said. "I thought that finally, at last, I had someone forever."

As though knocked over by the words, Lacey rolled back along the cabin floor. Her eyes followed the framing up, up, twenty feet up to where the apex pierced the crisp

November sky. Sixteen arrows aimed into forever. A late, clinging poplar leaf broke soundlessly from a limb and dipped and drifted down, down. Lacey's eyes followed the yellow, tulip-shaped leaf as it fell past the apex—dying, turning away from forever. The leaf fell onto her chest and slid to the cabin floor.

After another moment she said, "I thought so, too." Finally, she cried.

And Campbell stopped crying.

Moving

WOULD THE MIDDLE OF MONTHS ALWAYS BE HARD, Lacey wondered? Two months, now, since David had been killed, right there, so publicly, on the square. It didn't help when Bradley mustered the courage to say, "I'm sorry about your father." She just walked away.

The iron leaves and flowers were in boxes and on the table near the forge. Tulip-shaped poplar leaves, like the one that had pierced her chest and released her tears. Oak, maple, sourwood, all three leaves of sassafras. And, yes, trillium, the blossom nestled at the vortex of the three iron leaves. In her love for David and her need for busyness, she kept them dusted, turning them over and over in her hands. The only thing he was stern about was keeping a neat shop. That's where good commissions come from, he said. What would become of them, she wondered, these pieces for this commission?

Thumbtacked to the table, his sketch reminded her of what he meant to do. The outline of mountains rose and fell. Leaves and flowers drifted down. Lacey smiled at how David could make iron drift.

"Can't we make the balustrade?" she asked. She knew the basic techniques of how to do it, which didn't mean she could do it. But she could help. Campbell was a fine blacksmith. David had said.

"Lacey," Campbell said. "Don't start."

"Well, I wish you would start," Lacey said. "Start something." She stomped as well as one could stomp on a dirt floor. Not satisfied, she huffed and left the barn. Gravel turning underfoot was better. She ran, wishing it would spit out from under her shoes as it did from under car tires. She hoisted herself to the cabin floor and wondered what they would do. They were living on the down payment for the leaf-and-floral railing. She had thought that when Campbell stopped crying, she would start back to work. But day after day, Lacey came home to find that all Campbell had done was sit or walk. Paths were worn, now, around the edges of the property, around both the outside and inside of the pasture fence, around the barn, along both sides of the creek.

What could she do? She was only twelve years old. She could make nails, but nails were one of the least expensive

126

things at the hardware store. She could make belts and billfolds, but only slowly. A garden couldn't be planted until spring. Would they, after all this time, wind up at Grandmom's after all?

Harris's truck turned onto the road. As he clattered across the board bridge, he glanced toward the cabin. Lacey waved both arms and turned the wave into a summons. Harris turned toward the cabin and parked.

"Well, what's Miss Lacey contemplating from the cabin deck?" he asked.

She patted the floor and he sat, assuming her cross-legged position, and his knees went out like enormous chicken wings.

"You keep asking Campbell about finishing the cabin," Lacey said. The materials, covered with plastic, were stacked beside the cabin.

"And she keeps thanking me and saying 'no.' "

"Well, why don't we do it?" Lacey said. "Me and you."

"She doesn't want it touched."

"We're touching it now," she said.

He didn't respond. They both knew that wasn't what Campbell meant. Lacey looked at him with a combination of pleading and irritation. His Adam's apple was moving, even though his mouth wasn't. She suddenly remembered the day she had fled from the Gas and Gro. and walked home with a lump of fear in her throat. That was it, the lump. Harris was trying to swallow a lump in his throat.

"Lace bug," he said, "there's nothing I'd like to do more than finish this cabin." One of his eyes seemed to twinkle

127

from excess moisture and a spark glinted from it and hit Lacey with the power of a poplar leaf. Lace bug, he had called her.

How had she not known that he had suffered over David's death, too? David was his friend. She had been so busy with her own grief that she hadn't seen his. "Oh, Harri-i-isss," she cried, and she hugged him as tightly as she ever had Campbell or David. Under the baggy overalls, he was just as thin as he looked. "Are you kin to Marlene?" she asked, moving back with a sniff.

"No. Why?"

"Because you're both such skinny beans."

They sat and planned just what needed to be done and how they could manage to do it. "You can help me frame in the doors and windows," he said, "but I'll have to have more help than just you with that siding. It's heavy." They'd hopped off the deck and uncovered the materials to take stock. She tugged at a piece of the siding to prove to him she could handle it. She couldn't.

"It *is* heavy," she said.

"What if Campbell objects?" Harris said.

Another memory from that lump-in-the-throat day popped to the surface. "What," she said, with David-reason, "is the worst possible thing that could happen? Would she kill you?"

Harris laughed. "No. I don't guess she would. Maybe it would help her get off her—" He stopped as though he'd said something wrong.

"—butt," Lacey finished.

128

He laughed again. "I was going to say duff," he said. In a minute, he said, "Let's give it Sundays."

The very next Sunday, there was a wonderful clattering and banging on the floor deck of the cabin. Campbell didn't help. Campbell didn't even come to look. But she didn't say "stop," either. She took her boundary walks, and Harris and Lacey paused a moment and watched her grow smaller in the distance.

Lacey helped measure, handed lumber, held lumber, handed saw, nails, hammer. For most measurements, Harris said within a quarter of an inch would do. But for one that he said needed to be exact, she counted the smallest marks on the measuring tape and announced, "Four feet and thirteen-sixteenths of an inch."

"Oh, come on, Lacey. Thirteen-sixteenths. That's a ridiculous number." He took the measure from her and stretched it across where one of the four-foot windows was going.

"You said it had to be exact," she said.

He started laughing. She didn't like him laughing just because she'd measured wrong.

"It really is thirteen-sixteenths," he said, and he kept on laughing.

A giggle of relief popped out of her. "Oh, come on, Harris," she said. "That's a ridiculous number."

Even the weather cooperated. Seventy degrees and sunny in late December. "This is the South," Lacey said.

"Going to drop tonight, though," Harris said. "Supposed

to go down to twenty." Twenty was nothing compared to Colorado, but they had put on their jackets before sundown. "I don't know about you," Harris said at last. "But I can't see what I'm doing." Lacey was surprised to see that dark had grown up around them. "Next Sunday, then," he said as he left.

Lacey sat with her arms curled about her knees, looking at the new silhouettes in the structure. In just one day, they'd framed all the downstairs windows. She heard the truck and looked up. Time for her to go, too. She was on her feet, off the cabin floor, and heading for the bridge, when Campbell stopped.

"Lacey, come *on,*" Campbell said, as though she'd called fourteen times.

With an uh-oh bouncing around inside, Lacey ran. Campbell was mad because they'd worked on the cabin. As soon as she closed the truck door, Campbell spun off. Lacey grabbed for the seat belt and fastened it, something she always did now, since David. At the paved road, Campbell turned left, heading toward Bitter Creek and home, driving like Grandmom had that day she'd passed the school bus. The headlights cleared a path through the dark.

"What's wrong with you?" Lacey asked. She was sure she knew. Campbell wanted every board of the cabin untouched, left as David had left it. "David wanted that cabin built."

"Lacey, shut up!"

With teeth gnashing, Lacey shut. She'd heard other people use the words "shut up" as casually as a cat napped, but they'd never been used in this family. Lacey felt slapped. As they passed the Gas and Gro., Campbell stomped the accelerator and the tires squealed. Lacey rechecked her seat belt.

"Lacey, I'm sorry," Campbell said, as soon as the lights of Bitter Creek disappeared behind them. She put a hand out and patted Lacey on the knee, but the voice still had a snap. "I just can't help it."

"I think you can help it," Lacey said through clenched teeth. "And it would help if you would tell me what is going on." Words, David would say, tell me with words.

As Campbell spun into the driveway to the house, Lacey could feel the tires gouge through gravel. The next hard rain would start a washout here. She followed Campbell into the house, to the doorway of the bedroom that Campbell had abandoned since David's death. Campbell waded into the stack of boxes in the corner, sturdy boxes that had brought their stuff from Colorado, boxes in which she transported her goods to craft festivals, except she hadn't been to any since they'd been here, though the mountain area had been full of festivals all summer and fall.

"Here," Campbell said, tossing boxes Lacey's way. "Pack."

"Pack?" Lacey said.

"Lacey, will you for once just do as I say without asking for reasons, explanations, and motivations? Pack." And she threw another box.

Lacey took four boxes and went to her room. David had taught her to always look for reasons, explanations, and motivations, except in cases of emergency. Was this an emergency? Pack, she told herself, and she forced her hands to strip the bed of its brightly striped sheets. She felt sapped of energy. If she didn't keep moving, all motion would stop. Fourteen years from now she would still be standing on this spot. When the sheets were folded and placed in a box, she told herself, Open a drawer. Without seeing the contents, she removed them and plunked them into the box. A poem from A. A. Milne's *Now We Are Six* came to mind. Two bears, who were opposites, suddenly began changing, each becoming like the other. Where had Campbell gotten this burst of energy, all this movement, all this action? Were she and Campbell changing places like the two bears? She lifted her clothes from the drawers and into the boxes and carried the boxes out into the cold.

From the kitchen came clattering sounds of silverware and utensils. Lacey went and stood in the doorway. "Colorado?" she asked, as she rubbed the cold from her hands. There had been plenty of moves like this where, with a whisk and a bang, they'd packed up and gone to a new apartment, a new house, a new town.

"Lacey, just shut up and help me with this mattress."

"Am I going to have to get used to those words now?"

"What words?" Campbell asked, rolling the mattress.

"Shut up," Lacey said, helping stand the mattress on end. Campbell didn't respond, and the two of them tugged the mattress to the door, to the truck. There was no fun in it as when Campbell had been rolled inside it, those months ago. With just the light from the porch, they traipsed

132

back and forth with boxes, then Campbell made a last check of the four rooms.

"What about David's stuff?" Lacey asked. The utility trailer, the blacksmithing tools, and all the leaves and flowers were at the barn.

"Lacey," Campbell said with a warning growl.

"You can growl at me all you want," Lacey said, backing away from the truck and fastening her feet to the ground. "I'm not getting in that truck until I know where we're going." Not, not, not, she hoped, Grandmom's. She would stand here forever, grow to the earth and become a tree. That was one way of making her own roots. She realized the stupidity of not having made this stand sooner. All of her belongings were now loaded onto the truck.

Campbell gritted teeth and shook her head, stared across space and, in a very disgusted voice, said, "We're moving to the barn."

"The barn?" Lacey said. A "hah" of surprised, delighted laughter burst out. "The barn?" She leaped and laughed and ran for the truck. Campbell still acted furious, but Lacey kept laughing. The barn! She loved barns, especially this barn, David's barn.

The night was going to be cold, but Lacey and Campbell knew how to stay warm in a barn. This time it was even easier than it had been in Colorado. They simply borrowed a few pieces of building materials from the cabin site and built a lean-to against the side of Pretty Polly's stall. As they worked by flashlight, lugging lumber, hammering to secure it, Lacey kept laughing.

"I'm glad you think it's so damn funny," Campbell said. Her tone of voice expressed extreme irritation, but almost in spite of herself, she smiled. By the time they'd stretched a ground cover beneath the lean-to and dragged the mattress in, Campbell was laughing, too. Rummaging through a box for food was funny. Making sandwiches in the dark was funny. Even the cold was funny. Here they were in a barn again, but this time it was David's barn, their barn.

The Ice Palace

"LACEY, WE DON'T HAVE A THING," CAMPBELL CON-
fessed in the night. They lay huddled together, listening
to the thump of Polly's movements in the adjacent stall.
"Mrs. Ford hasn't been paid her rent since October. We
had to move. She told me we had to move by the first of
the year. I didn't know what we were going to do. I was
just going to sit there and make her kick us out."

"Oh, Campbell," Lacey murmured.

"Then you and Harris, pounding on that cabin all day."
Campbell hugged Lacey. "You've got spunk, kiddo. Guts
and spunk." Her voice sounded a little choked, or was it
sleepiness?

"So do you," Lacey said. "And if you start crying again, I'm going to have the guts to—" She stopped, because she didn't know what. She pictured herself walking, walking, walking, not around the pasture or the edge of the property, but all the way to Colorado, being snowed on, and growing larger and larger as snow collected on her clothing.

"David made several property payments ahead, but they'll be due again soon. And it's not our property. I don't know how long we can stay here."

"It *is* ours," Lacey said. "David would want it to be ours."

Campbell hugged her again. "That's not the way the world works, Lacey."

"We'll have to make it work," Lacey said.

Morning was when they felt the cold. Wrapped in blankets, they toddled out from the shelter and started a fire. Campbell plugged the microwave into David's droplight extension cord and Lacey fished two mugs from the box of dishes. Looking from their huddle-shelter to the microwave, Lacey giggled, then Campbell laughed, too. Lacey's teeth clacked from laughter and from cold. It was ridiculous, she thought, to make hot chocolate in a microwave in the middle of this rough barn. If they could keep on laughing, though, they would be all right.

Shivering, even beneath the blanket, she wandered to the PEOPLE door and looked out. She expected snow, a thick white covering of the imperfections of the earth, as a symbol. There was only the tawny stubble of winter grass. It was too cold and dry even for frost. Crossing back to their stacks of boxes, she pulled clothes from a box and tucked them under the blanket to warm them before she put them on. Then, dressed and with her Mackinaw on top, she paced around the barn with her hands curved around a cup of hot chocolate. Polly stomped and stomped to keep herself warm.

Lacey heard Grandmom's honk and ran out. "I didn't see you go by," she said as Lacey climbed into the back seat this morning. "You must have come over early."

"We did," Lacey said, shuddering with relief at the warmth of the car and scarcely able to contain her amusement at how early they had come over. "We sure did."

At school, in the cafeteria, Tam came and sat with her. Lacey almost dropped her fork in surprise.

"I'm glad to see you happy again," Tam said.

Lacey stared at Tam. When David was killed, Tam had said, "I'm sorry about David," but nothing more, no other friendliness. How was it that Tam was able to detect this very day when Lacey did, in fact, feel happy?

"I hated seeing you so unhappy," Tam said.

I'll bet you did, Lacey thought, and she ground her teeth on a mouthful of dried limas. Exchanging friendly remarks with Tam was now an unfamiliar act. Some slender wishful thread tugged at her but the larger part of her resisted.

"Maybe I could come over," Tam said, and Lacey nearly toppled off the chair.

"I, uh, well. Uh." Why now, this very day, Lacey wanted to shout, after all the invitations in July and August and September? This was December. "I, uh, well." She knew that every word of hesitation was damaging Tam's efforts at friendliness, and she fumbled for a way to soften it, but she could not let Tam find out they were living at the barn. "I mean, well, there are reasons why you can't right now," she said. "It doesn't have anything to do with you and me." She was still trying to think how else to say it, when Tam's next words nearly made her fall through her chair instead of off it.

With a nodding head and a knowing look that was a replica of Grandmom's face, Tam said, "Uh-huh. Just like Grandmom says. I bet Campbell's already with another lover." And there wasn't a bit of love in the words.

When Lacey recovered enough to move, she picked up her tray, pushed her chair away from the table, and marched off toward the tray-return window.

"Lacey, are you all right?" someone said from behind her. It was Cheryl, not Tam, but she didn't turn around. She plunked her tray down without putting trash, silverware, garbage, glass in the proper places. In the office, she said "I have to use the phone" so forcefully that the student on duty didn't object, just pointed to it.

Please, please be home and not at the barn, she thought, and she was taken totally by surprise when a recording said, "The number you have dialed has been disconnected." Of course, of course, they had moved to the barn and there was no phone there. This was the first time she had needed to leave school and there was no one to come get her. David would have known by telepathy, she thought, but even as she thought it, she knew it wasn't true. If he'd been alive and at the barn, she wouldn't have been able to reach him, either.

She walked out of the junior high building and across the school grounds to the adjacent elementary school building. The bulletin board looked as ragged and sorry as it had last year. She pushed open the door to the office, saw Mr. Palmer's door open, and walked right in.

"Hello, Lacey," he said.

"Will you take me home?" she asked. "I mean, to the barn? Campbell's at the barn, so I can't call her to come get me."

"May I call your grandmother?" he asked, reaching for the phone on his desk.

"No," she said.

"All right, Lacey." He stood up to go. "Do they know over at the school?" She shook her head. "I'll call and tell them so they won't be worried, so you won't be in trouble." He dialed, spoke, identified himself, and said she needed to be excused for the rest of the day.

She followed him out of his office, through the outer office, past the scruffy bulletin board, and to his small brown car that was parked in a spot marked PRINCIPAL. All the way home she waited for the questions to begin. They did not. She could learn to like a person who didn't ask questions, she thought. He drove onto the gravel road, across the plank bridge, up next to Campbell's truck by the barn, and tooted the horn once, as a signal.

"Thank you very much," she said as she got out.

"You're very welcome, Lacey," he said, then he backed, turned, and drove away.

Campbell came in response to the sound of the car, and Lacey ran and flung arms around her.

"I'm not riding with them anymore. You'll just have to take me if you don't want the school bus stopping for me."

"What in the world, sweetheart?" Campbell rubbed Lacey's back, arms, and hair. "What's happened to my laughing girl?"

Grandmom insistently appeared every morning for the next four days, and Campbell just as insistently drove Lacey to school. Tam never even looked at Lacey and one morning Grandmom said, "What's wrong with you two?" Ridgewire was slow. It was Saturday before Grandmom came roaring up the road, spitting gravel off the tires, and Lacey knew she knew about them living at the barn. Lacey was in the pasture with Polly and she came galloping toward the paddock. Grandmom stopped dead center on the narrow bridge, left the car door open, and stalked up the road in yard-long steps.

"So I have to find out these things from Reba Ford," Grandmom said. Lacey saw Campbell at the PEOPLE WITH HORSES door. "How are Campbell and Lacey getting along, she says. I say fine, I just wish they'd come live with us, that's all. And she says, where are they living, then?" Grandmom flipped up the gate latch and marched into the paddock instead of going through the PEOPLE door. She hiked past Campbell and into the barn.

As Lacey slid off Polly, she felt the foal kick. She rubbed

Polly's side and murmured sweet horse-talk as she opened the gate between pasture and paddock and led Polly through.

"What do you think you're doing?" Grandmom was saying, feet wide, hands on hips, as though to take up as much space as possible. She was staring at the lean-to.

Lacey noticed the basket-weave design tool in Campbell's hand and looked beyond the lean-to. There was a piece of saddle on the worktable and a fire in the forge, for warmth.

"Campbell!" Lacey said. Campbell glanced at Lacey, followed Lacey's eyes, held up the tool, and nodded. Lacey didn't care what Grandmom said. The foal was kicking strong and Campbell was back at work.

"And in this weather," Grandmom said.

"Damn inconsiderate of David to get himself killed in autumn instead of spring," Campbell said.

"The very idea," Grandmom said, clicking and hissing like a combination of a chicken and a snake. Lacey opened the door to the stall and swatted Polly on the rump to get her to go in. Before Pretty Polly moved herself through the doorway, she plopped two pods of fresh manure. Hands still on hips, Grandmom pretended to walk around the lean-to, though there was really nothing one could walk around.

"Tomato, Potato, Vegetable, Split Pea." Grandmom reeled off names of soups like curse words. "This is the most headstrong, insane thing I've ever heard of."

"We're managing," Campbell said.

"We're managing fine," Lacey added.

"Lacey, you stay out of it," Campbell said quietly.

With a nasty, nodding, knowing look, Grandmom said, "Look what you're doing to this child."

"She's not doing anything to me," Lacey said.

"Lacey, you stay out of it," Grandmom said loudly.

"I will not stay out of it," Lacey said. She stepped over to Campbell's worktable and rubbed the newly imprinted design. "This is my life you're talking about. I'm old enough to speak up for myself and I like it here."

"She's got you talking crazy, too," Grandmom said. "She's brainwashed you into this stupid, immoral life-style."

Campbell lifted a bucket of water and threw it onto the fire. As the hiss of steam rose, Campbell said, "Let's go, Lacey."

"You can't get out," Grandmom said. Double-checking the stall gate as they went by, Campbell and Lacey walked out.

"You can't get out," Grandmom repeated. "I have you blocked in." By that time Lacey, following Campbell, had latched both paddock gates and realized she had shut Grandmom in. She almost turned to reverse the procedure. Closing and latching those gates was as automatic as breathing. But Campbell was already in the truck, and Lacey hopped in the other side.

"Don't you just walk off from me," Grandmom was saying, unlatching the barn-to-paddock gate.

With a backup and a whirl-turn, Campbell was heading for the bridge. She stopped bumper to bumper with the Buick and ordered Lacey out. Without asking for reasons, explanations, or motivations, Lacey jumped out. Campbell climbed across the bumpers to the driver's side of the open-doored car. "Get in," she said to Lacey.

Me? Lacey thought, but she got.

"Put your foot on the brake pedal and when I'm in the truck, just ease it off and let her roll back."

Grandmom was coming through the second paddock gate now, no snake, just squawking chicken.

Campbell popped the gear indicator to Neutral and released the parking brake. "When I drive around the car, you press the pedal to reset the parking brake. Then come on! No time for wasted motion."

Hands on steering wheel, foot hard against the brake pedal, Lacey waited until Campbell was back in the truck. Then she eased up the brake and the truck pushed the car as smooth and easy as anything, without even a jerk. When Campbell pulled up alongside the car, Lacey stomped the regular brake pedal with one foot and the parking brake pedal with the other. When she scrambled from the Buick, she left the door open the way it had been.

Campbell raced up the road away from Bitter Creek, toward Savory, past Savory, up through the mountains toward Logan. "If anyone is crazy," she spoke at last, "you know who it is, don't you?"

After another while, Lacey asked, "How did you learn to do that?"

"What?"

"Push cars."

"Lacey, my dear. I can do almost anything."

At the top of the mountain, there was the Ice Palace! Campbell pulled over and stopped. Cascades of ice transformed the steep rock walls into huge white sheets and stalactites and stalagmites. The sun glinting off it was brighter than off water.

"Ablaze with ice," Lacey said, remembering Campbell's description of the cliffs. She slipped out of the truck and walked over to the ice wall. Campbell followed. They placed their palms against the wall of the palace until their hands were frozen. Lacey looked at Campbell and smiled. This was not a place for laughing. This was a place for being quiet in, Campbell's Ice Palace.

Campbell set a cold hand on Lacey's cheek and returned the smile and said, "I love you, Old Lace."

Dancing

THE CABIN WENT UP BY SUNDAYS. FLAG CORPS WAS over and the year turned as Lacey and Harris framed for the doors and the loft windows. They had no more funny numbers like thirteen-sixteenths, but they laughed a lot.

Though Campbell was pleased, now, that the work was going on, she still stayed away, up at the barn. She was almost finished with the saddle and had sent a description of it to friends in Colorado in case the man who ordered it was no longer waiting.

"I know someone who would like to help me with the siding," Harris said.

"Great," Lacey said, before she realized he hadn't finished.

"I asked Campbell about it and she said to check with you."

"Well, sure, sure. What's to check? Is it someone I know?" She was on the third rung of the ladder from where she'd just held the top of the door frame for him to nail in place. Their eyes were on a level and he was looking at her carefully, curiously. She felt the uh-oh before he said the name.

"It's Wally Palmer."

Lacey was so stunned she couldn't even say "Oh." It was almost as hard to hear that Wally Palmer was alive as it had been to hear that David was dead. And Harris had told her both things.

"Well," she said, wanting to say "Sure," but it wouldn't come out. She had known he was alive, of course, technically alive, but he had never been alive to her. There were those wavery moments last spring when she'd met Fred Palmer, the fear that Wally would materialize and try to claim something, but it didn't happen.

Now Harris had said his name right here in the cabin. She looked down. No cutout letters spelled the name Wally Palmer across the floor. There was just the brown, weathered plywood with various crisscrossings of their footprints. Which footprints were David's? She wished now she had thought to outline his footprints in ink.

"Well?" Harris said. "I don't want it to be anything that upsets you. He doesn't want it to be anything that upsets you. He said he doesn't want to intrude on your life at this late date, but that he'd like to do this small thing for you."

146

Her mind skipped and skidded over all the other people who might come help, but it didn't stop on any. Kenny and Grandpop were the closest kin and also lived the nearest, but they hadn't said one word about helping. The people they'd known at the Craft School were totally out of their lives. They were exactly the sort of people who would have helped, but she and Campbell had let themselves disappear. They hadn't been to the Craft School once since David's death, not for one dance. She was the one who'd got the work started again on the cabin and this person, Wally Palmer, wanted to help. That's all he was, a person who wanted to help. Someone Campbell had known once. That's all.

"Sure," she said, thinking the word had traveled fourteen miles to get from her throat to her lips.

So Wally Palmer came. Campbell stayed where she always did, in the barn, working on the saddle. Awkwardness was thick on the cabin deck, but Harris had them working pretty quickly. Climbing twenty feet up the ladder and hoisting heavy sheets of 4 x 8's didn't allow Wally much time for chatter. Except for being tall, he didn't look anything like Fred Palmer.

During rest break, Wally said, "I have a son and a daughter. Ten and eight."

Lacey's teeth and everything else within her clenched.

"I have to go feed Polly," she said, and she jumped down through the framed doorway and clacked up gravel to the barn. She didn't want to hear about his children. She didn't want to think about being his child. Except for helping put the siding on this cabin, she wanted him in the invisible background where he'd been for the past twelve years.

"How's it going?" Campbell asked, when Lacey appeared in the barn.

"Mmmmm," Lacey said, picking up a piece of chamois cloth. She wanted Campbell in the background, too. She wound the cloth around her knuckles and attacked one of the stirrups on Polly's saddle, to polish it. Feeding Polly was a "flat-out" lie. A horse was fed morning and evening, never in the middle of the day, unless it was grazing. Hammer sounds from the cabin rang in her ears and she wanted to be back, wanted to watch every nail hit home. Having made such an abrupt exit, though, she didn't know how to go back. She didn't want to hear Wally say one thing that would make him seem familiar and real. She did not want to see one thing of herself in him as she did in Campbell and in Grandmom. She finished polishing the stirrups and sauntered casually back to the cabin, as though watching them put up the siding was the least important thing of her day. Wally carefully avoided looking at her, but she kept looking at him until he felt her gaze and returned it.

"Let's just don't talk about it, okay?" she said. As he looked back at her, she wondered what he saw. Did he see Ann Campbell Bittner, whom he used to take to school? Did he see Eva Bittner, who tried to stop him? When he had spoken of his son and daughter, he had not said he had *another* daughter, as though he were counting her, too.

He looked at her and nodded and said, "Okay," and she

148

knew he didn't see a daughter standing there inside her skin any more than she saw a father standing there. David was still her father. Wally had come to help Harris with the cabin. That was enough.

Late one afternoon during the week, they heard the sound of tires on gravel, looked out, and here came Kenny, driving his pickup to the paddock fence and walking in through the PEOPLE door.

"I just come by to see how y'all are," he said, avoiding looking at the lean-to by walking past it toward Campbell's leatherwork. "And to see if you won't come on to dinner Sunday."

Lacey was surprised at her pleasure in his seeking them out and asking. He hadn't been to the barn since the last time David had the Sunday dinner here at the end of September. She and Campbell hadn't been to Sunday dinner in a month.

"Harris is helping us with the cabin on Sundays," Campbell said.

A "ha!" burst out of Lacey at the way Campbell included herself in on the cabin. If Campbell had even been down to see it, it had been while Lacey was at school. "You mean *we're* helping Harris," she said, pleased with herself for getting two layers of meaning into the remark, one for Kenny and another for Campbell.

"Well, you have to eat," Kenny said.

"But I don't have to be called cream of potato," Campbell said.

Kenny was looking at the saddle, which was put together

now and looked like a saddle, not just bits and pieces of leather. "Campbell, this is a damn handsome saddle," he said, stroking the leather. "What do you call this pattern?" He ran his fingers along it.

"Basket-weave," Campbell said.

"Sure. I should have known that. That's just what it looks like. Pretty." He wandered toward the forge and looked at the iron leaves and flowers on David's table, but he didn't touch them. "Tam's out yonder in the truck," he said, extending a thumb and flicking it truckward. Lacey followed the trajectory as though she could see through the barn wall to the truck. "She wouldn't come in." He walked back over and rubbed the saddle again, lifting the stirrup leather, then the fender. "I wish to hell I knew what was going on in this family."

Campbell walked toward David's table now, away from Kenny. She picked up a metal maple leaf and set it back down, then a blackjack oak leaf and put it down.

"Kenny," she said, turning toward him. "I'm just trying to live my life."

Standing by the lean-to, Lacey tensed, waiting for Kenny's response. At least he hadn't parked on the bridge. They wouldn't have to push his truck out of the way if they decided to flee to the Ice Palace.

Kenny continued his examination of the saddle, touching the skirt and the back jockey. Then he sighed. "I know," he said. "And it seems you're doing a damn fine job of it."

Lacey started to say that how they lived their lives was none of his business, but Campbell had said his name in a soft and tender tone. Lacey looked quickly from brother to sister, her mother the sister.

"How do you do this?" Kenny asked.

"It's an imprinting stamp," Campbell said, walking over, picking it up, showing him the end of it and how she tapped the design into the leather.

Lacey was surprised. What she'd taken as a sarcastic remark apparently wasn't, and after all these years Campbell still knew her brother well enough.

"It's done you good to get away," he said. "You're living life on your own terms." He bobbed his head slightly. "I've just stayed right here. And I'm still Kenny Tom."

The next Sunday afternoon, Kenny and Grandpop came around to help work on the cabin.

"Need an extra hand or two?" Kenny called out.

"Sure do," Harris said. They'd put up the lowest siding first, so it would provide a narrow ledge to balance the next row on. Harris and Wally were just fastening on the top row of siding. Harris looked down at Kenny. "There's umpty tubes of caulk and ever who wants to can start beading the seams."

"Awww," said Lacey, who'd wanted to caulk and been refused the job.

"Who's your helper?" Kenny asked, as Harris and Wally descended from the ladder. "I'm Kenny Bitt—" Hand extended and half his name still in his mouth, Kenny recognized Wally. "Wally Palmer?" He put the question mark at the end, but Lacey knew he had no question. Kenny's dark eyes darkened more and she saw hate spring to his face. He rubbed his hands on his jeans and shoved them in his pockets as if to keep them from flying out. What, Lacey wondered, did these two have between them? "Wally Palmer, I could still beat the shit out of you with pleasure."

"Come on, Kenny. It's been twelve years," Wally said.

"Twelve years don't make no difference in Bitter Creek," Kenny said.

Just as she was about to be amused at the comical aspects of the exchange, it dawned on Lacey that what they had between them was her.

"Kenny-y-y," she said. "He's not my father. He's just a person who has come to help work on the cabin, okay?"

Kenny looked dubious.

She looked at Wally Palmer, whose genes were in her whether she saw evidence of them or not. "Right, Wally?" she asked.

With a quick grin Wally said, "Right."

"Okay?" she said to Kenny.

Kenny didn't agree it was okay, but he picked up a tube of caulk, slit the plastic cap with his pocketknife, popped the tube into the caulk gun, and started zapping a seam between pieces of siding, climbing the ladder slowly as he went.

"Where'd you learn to be such a diplomat?" Wally asked. "Not from your Uncle Kenny, surely."

"From David," she said instantly.

Wally came just those two Sundays. He'd come to help with the siding and the siding was done.

Grandpop and Kenny came other Sundays, after dinner. Grandpop, visiting Campbell and Polly in the barn, said, "Come spring, I'd like to have you board me a horse, if the offer is still open."

"Oh, Papa, yes," Campbell said.

In two more weeks, all the caulking was done, the roof cap was on, and the doors and most of the windows were in. Harris had a surprise window in his truck, wrapped in a blanket.

"I wish I could send you off so you wouldn't see it until it was in place, but I need help with it, and you should be the one to help and the one to see it first, before your granddad and Kenny get here."

She helped him carry it to the cabin, still blanket-wrapped. They hoisted it into place before he let the blanket fall away. This window, in the spot David had picked so it would look out on the trillium, was full of trillium. A large center pane was clear glass, but around the edges, in stained glass, was every kind of trillium there was.

"For you and Campbell," Harris said, "but especially for David."

"Where did you get it?" she asked when she had tongue enough.

"I made it."

"You made it?"

"Sure. That's what I do when I'm not building cabins."

"I'll go get Campbell," she said, running up the gravel. Why had she never wondered what Harris did when he wasn't being their friend? She interrupted Campbell's work by saying, "Come. You have to come." She held out her hand, ready to plead, badger, command, or pitch a fit if need be, but Campbell asked for no reasons, explanations, or motivations. They walked back down the driveway holding hands, and Campbell came to the cabin site for the first time since work had resumed.

"Oh, Harris," Campbell said when she saw the window. "Oh, Harris. Oh, Harris."

When the others had gone that Sunday, Campbell and Lacey dragged the floppy mattress to the truck and took it to the cabin and slept there, laughing and talking into the night as much as they had the night they'd moved into the barn.

The next Saturday night, they returned to the folk dance. They were late and the music reached out to the wooded parking lot like welcoming arms. Through the windows, they could see dancers moving up and down a contra line. Lacey was amazed at how happy she was to be here. She took hold of Campbell's hand as they walked the curve of driveway. Campbell was working again. Campbell was in motion.

The contra ended as they walked inside, and two men they knew immediately saw Campbell and moved toward her, holding out a hand as invitation for the next dance. Seeing that two of them were approaching, one of them bowed and held his hand to Lacey instead. She shook her head, as always. They all knew she didn't dance, she only watched, and they hardly ever asked her anymore. This was just a glad-you're-back gesture.

154

Yet she didn't want to sit, either. She dreaded having people coming up and saying sympathetic things. Some of these people knew what a special person David was. She walked into the hallway to the water fountain, but there was a line, those who were taking a water break between dances. She meandered onto the deck and stared at the black trees against the black night.

When she heard music again, she wandered back into the dance room and sat down. The dance was another contra and, as she watched, she realized that she wished she was out there, dancing. When they'd first returned to Bitter Creek and come to the dances, David had kept asking her to dance. Then he had said, "Let me know when you're ready, Lace."

David, I'm ready now, she thought, but David was not there to take her hand.

The next dance announced was Nine Pins. This was one of Tam's favorites, she knew. The dance required four couples in a square and an extra person in the middle. Tam never wanted a partner for this dance, she always ran to be that ninth pin in the middle. Before she thought, Lacey jumped up and darted to the center of one of the squares. Once there, she regretted her impulse, felt like a fool, and was tempted to run right out again, but that would make her feel like more of a fool.

In this place where she'd spent so many Saturday nights, she felt like a stranger. The couple in front of her and the pair on each side were people she didn't know. She turned slowly, to see who was behind her and there, his body hiding behind the loose overalls, was Harris.

"May I borrow a hair clip, Lacey?" he asked, and he moved his fingers and began braiding his beard.

Patricia Lamb called out the instructions and Lacey let them flow over her head. She knew her part in this dance. The head couples would cross and try to bowl her over, then the side couples would do the same. Her job was to dodge. At one point, there would be a move like musical chairs or applecart turnover, which would be her chance to snare a partner, and whoever was left without a partner became the center pin. The music started and Lacey dodged skillfully. Then just as skillfully, she did not grab a partner.

The second time the music stopped, Harris reached out and caught her as she was trying to bumble her way out of catching a partner. Now she realized that she didn't know what the side and head couples did. He quickly showed her, holding her hands and stretching them out to left and right as far as her arms would reach. He was taller, even, than she'd thought! With sliding steps, they sashayed across the set, pretending to try to bowl over the center pin, who dodged. Having a partner for the dance was just as much fun, she discovered, as being the lone ninth pin. She was not graceful, but she was dancing.

When the dance was over, Harris kept hold of her hand. "Next dance?" he asked.

"I might not know it," she said.

"They'll teach it," he said.

"I guess," she said. It was a wonderful complicated dance called Symmetrical Squares, which involved going down the hall in lines of four, with two people ducking under an arch made by the other two. Watching Harris duck was pretty funny. All four holding hands and sort of tied in a half knot, they shuffled back up the hall, tangled themselves more before they untangled and moved on to the next couple. They were couples with Kenny and Tam once and Lacey said, "Next dance?" to Tam.

With no hesitation at all, Tam said, "Oh, yes."

She danced with Tam, then Kenny, then Tina, and Marlene, and Campbell, and she didn't sit out another dance.

Equal Partners

A MAN CAME FROM ASHEVILLE LOOKING FOR DAVID. He was in the driveway when Campbell brought Lacey home from school.

"Are you Mrs. Habib?" he asked, when they got out by the cabin.

"I'm Campbell Bittner," Campbell said. "David and I worked together. We were partners."

Lacey was proud of Campbell for saying that. If it wasn't a technical, legal fact, it was nonetheless true.

"I wish someone had informed me of his death," the man said. "We have been waiting for the railing, trying to get in touch with him."

158

Lacey glanced toward the barn as though parts and pieces of the leaf-and-floral railing could be seen from here.

"We still want it. How near finished was he? Can you recommend someone who could complete his work?"

Campbell and Lacey looked at one another, nodded to each other and to the man, and started walking toward the barn. We could finish it, she wanted to say, but she knew he wouldn't take the word of a twelve-year-old. They'd been living on this man's money, the down payment for the railing. They'd been spending only for gas and food. Campbell had gotten food stamps.

The man chuckled over the PEOPLE and PEOPLE WITH HORSES signs.

"That was David's idea," Campbell said, and she smiled.

"Yeah, that was David's idea," Lacey said, happy to see Campbell mention David and smile.

"Ah, beautiful, beautiful, just what we wanted," the man said, fingering dogwood, fire pink, all three leaves of sassafras. His fingers and eyes traced the drawing on the table, a drawing he had a copy of. "Can I take what he has finished and pay a prorated price to his estate?"

"We can finish it," Campbell said. Lacey bit her lip to contain an exclamation of joy. "I'm sorry we didn't contact you. That was wrong of me, but—" She shrugged and held out hands of apology. "I was distraught, and sort of let things go, and I didn't know if you would trust the work of a woman."

The man looked as though he wasn't sure himself. "You **say** you worked with him?"

159

"Equal partners," Campbell said. "He said I was almost as good as he was, and he's done the most difficult part." She indicated the leaves and flowers and the four-foot sections of the outlines of the mountains. "Basically, it's forming the balustrade to feel just right to the hand, and rounding the balusters, then welding it all together."

"Can you handle that part? Seems like heavy work."

"I can get all the help I need," Campbell said, and she did not look at Lacey.

"When could we expect delivery? We're already running late."

Lacey looked at Campbell as though her mother's eyes were calculators and the figures would roll across the eyeballs. She wanted to prompt. She wondered if Campbell remembered about the project, how many balusters there were, how many David had done, how long it took to do each one.

"Six weeks," Campbell said. "You can expect delivery in six weeks, firm. Can you stand to wait six weeks more? I don't know of anyone who could do it sooner."

"Six weeks," the man said. "Yes. I guess we'll have to. We certainly can't afford to start over. As his partner, you should have let us know, of course, but these things happen, and we have to start from where we are today."

Lacey held her breath while they finished the conversation. Polly snickered and stomped, unhappy to have people in the barn without having her usual after-school attention.

"You have a horse?" the man asked.

160

"Of course," Lacey said. "What's a barn for?"

Looking at the leatherwork and the forge, the man laughed. "Looks like this barn is for all sorts of fine things." As he walked by Polly's stall, he stroked her muzzle. "In foal?" he asked.

"Nine or ten more weeks," Campbell said.

"You're a lucky little girl," he said. "I always wanted a horse."

"Then why don't you have one?" Lacey asked.

"That's a good question," he said, and he walked out the PEOPLE door and back down to his car.

"I'll quit school to help," Lacey immediately said.

"You'll do no such thing, Lacey Bittner."

"School makes me miss everything," Lacey said.

"I don't think you miss much, Miss Lacey-puss."

Rains came steady and long, and made it good to be inside toasting by the forge. Lacey spent her afternoons and weekends there even when there was nothing, really, she could do. With tongs, Campbell held rod after rod to the fire until the end was cherry red, then she pushed it through the die to round it off. Then she heated the middle and pushed it through, then reversed ends and rounded the other end. There were a dozen balusters per four-foot section, and the entire railing was to be one hundred and twelve feet long. David had designed the mountain outline and the arrangement of leaves and flowers to repeat every four sections, which was seven repeats.

"Lacey, what would you think about riding to and from

school with Grandmom again?" Campbell asked one evening when, both of them black, they were scrubbing with Goop.

"You mean ask her?" Lacey said, feeling kicked.

"I'll ask her, if you'll agree to it," Campbell said. "Some days, I really can't take the time to come get you. And I need you here sooner than you could get here on the school bus."

Lacey knew the truth of everything Campbell was saying. She wanted Campbell at the forge and she wanted to be there herself every minute she could. At school and at the dances, she was friends again with Tam, but she hadn't even seen Grandmom in two and a half months. Tam's hurtful words that day in the school lunchroom were, she knew, Grandmom's words.

"Would it help if we went to Sunday dinner a couple times first?"

"Maybe," Lacey said.

And so they went, and Grandmom started right in.

"So, Turkey Noodle is finally back again," Grandmom said. As usual, they'd started serving their plates as soon as the grandparents had crossed the road.

"Well, I'm very glad they're here, Hortense," Tam said.

Lacey almost dropped the serving spoon full of string beans.

"Who are you calling Hortense, girl?" Kenny asked, though everyone knew.

Tam was at the head of the line. She put a slice of cherry cheescake on her plate and headed for the table.

"Tam?" Kenny asked.

"I just don't think it's very nice to call people by names they don't like," Tam said. Lacey was now at the cheesecake and she dreaded turning toward the table.

"Is that why you did it?" Kenny said. "You don't like to be nice?" All of them but Tam were standing along the serving line as if they were carved out of stone. Worse than watching was being part of this frieze. Lacey stepped toward the table.

"Just because she's the oldest doesn't give her the right to be rude to our company," Tam said, alone at the table.

"I am not the oldest," Grandmom said. "Tom's the oldest."

"Now, Eva," Grandpop said.

"Tam," Kenny said, "I think you'd better go to your room."

As graceful as a dancer, Tam rose, almost with a bow. "I'll be happy to go to my room," she said.

"Tam, honey, take your plate," Marlene said. "You shouldn't have to go hungry."

As Tam picked up her plate and moved toward the bedroom wing, Campbell came off the end of the line with cheesecake on her plate. "Tam, I'll be happy to go to your room, too," she said, and she followed Tam out of the room.

"Me, too," Lacey said, picking up a glass of tea as she went.

"Me, too," said Teresa very loudly, and she trailed Lacey.

163

Tam set her plate on her desk and Campbell perched hers on the top of the dresser. Lacey stood holding hers until Teresa, looking for a place, put her plate and herself on the floor.

"Me, too," said Lacey, and she sat beside Teresa. Teresa giggled at Lacey and Lacey giggled back. Campbell stepped over their legs and closed the door just in time to add to the laughter.

"Hortense!" Lacey said, and that got Tam started, and none of them could eat for laughing. They stopped fast when the door opened and there stood Grandmom.

"I'm glad you're having such a good time," she said.

Teresa giggled again.

"I will stop calling you Soup if Tam will stop calling me Hortense. Agreed?" Grandmom said.

How cleverly Grandmom worded it, Lacey thought, making it sound as though Tam had called Grandmom Hortense as many times as Grandmom had called Campbell soup names. As though it were that simple.

"All right," Campbell said, and Lacey swallowed so fast she choked.

After several "Are you all rights?" to which Lacey nodded, Grandmom spoke to Campbell again. "What may I call you, then? I just can't call you Campbell. Can't I please call you Ann, as I always have?"

"I never asked you to stop calling me Ann," Campbell said. Lacey felt her eyes bulge. Could it really be that simple?

"Will you all please come back to the table?"

"Sure," Campbell said.

"Sure," Teresa said, and those two started out.

Lacey wasn't sure she could move. Grandmom had conceded and said "please" twice in one minute.

"Tam?" Grandmom said, and Lacey understood that it was not that simple. The trigger here was Tam, the treasured, favorite granddaughter, and not the daughter at all. The concession was to Tam, not to Campbell. Tam was looking at Lacey now, waiting for Lacey's response. Lacey wasn't sure she wanted to make amends, but the look of pain on Tam's face was terrible.

"It *is* more comfortable at the table," Lacey said, and she lifted her plate, her glass, and herself.

"Tam?" Grandmom said again, as Lacey squeezed by Grandmom at the door. Lacey glanced back.

"Okay," Tam said slowly, and for one long moment Lacey thought Tam was going to add, "Hortense."

"Welcome back," Grandmom said when they were all reseated. "I'm glad you decided to quit being silly and come back to the table."

Lacey realized they had given Grandmom power by letting her settle it. Or, she thought, the illusion of power. Just because someone thought they had power over you didn't mean they had it. She looked at Tam and wanted to hug her, but that was too much siding up. Instead, she reached out to Teresa, who was next to her, and teasingly, lovingly, tugged at her hair.

The pull of hair pulled a giggle right up out of Teresa and that high-pitched, innocent laughter started them again. Even Grandmom was hooked into it until all but Kenny, Marlene, and Grandpop were laughing like fools.

Trillium

BY THE CALENDAR IT WAS SPRING AGAIN, BUT EXCEPT for pines and pipsissewa, which held green against every onslaught of winter, the earth was still brown. As they completed the leaf-and-flower railing, Lacey kept two of the pieces, a trillium for Campbell and a fire pink for herself. The trillium, which included the trifoil leaves, was more than six inches in diameter, but the fire pink was the flower alone and Lacey could carry it in her pocket. And she carried it there while she folk-danced, while she had Sunday dinner with the family, and while she rode to and from school again with Grandmom. It was like having a piece of David-luck in her pocket.

Afternoons and weekends, she helped Campbell with the railing, or fastened buckles to belts, or did finishing work on billfolds, preparing for the Craft School's Spring Festival. They were at the hard part of the railing now, with Campbell welding it together into four-foot sections that were awkward and heavy to handle.

"I wish I could afford to hire a young man to help hold and lift," Campbell said.

"Ask Harris," Lacey said.

"He's given so much to us already," Campbell said. "We can do it."

Some of the folk dancers were going to give a demonstration at the festival. Campbell and Lacey stayed after the dance for two Saturday nights, to practice. Tam wanted to be in it, too, and Campbell and Lacey took Tam home after practice.

The weekend of the festival was sunny and cool. Booths were set up along both sides and across one end of a large covered pavilion. There were all sorts of arts and crafts and demonstrations of arts and crafts, and all sorts of good things to eat. Outside, someone made lye soap, another made hominy, and there was a blacksmith working at a portable forge. Lacey was both drawn and repelled by the blacksmith. It was supposed to have been David, should have been David.

The center of the pavilion was for all sorts of musical entertainment, including the folk dancing. Along one end were bleacher-type seats where people could sit to eat the food they'd bought and watch the entertainment.

She helped at Campbell's booth. There were belts and billfolds for sale. Campbell had brought Polly's saddle to show, and had made a poster with photographs of her other saddles and information about having one custom-made. Lacey was used to this type of crafts fair from Colorado. It was such fun, seeing people she knew from the folk dances and from school.

Even Bradley.

"Your mother makes these?" he asked, fingering a belt imprinted with the basket-weave design.

"Yes," Lacey answered, "and I help."

The second day, Grandmom and Grandpop came, and they stopped by the booth, seeming pleased and proud. Lacey could still scarcely believe the mending had been so easy. Why, she wondered, had there been nearly a year of hostility first?

When the folk dance demonstration began, Grandmom and Grandpop stood on the fringes and watched. In one of the dances, Ms. Lamb taught the dance to the onlookers, then the partners were to separate and choose new partners from the audience. When it was time, Tam made straight for Grandmom. Almost as quickly, Lacey walked over and reached out for Grandpop.

"We haven't danced for years," Grandmom said, holding back a bit, but both of them allowed themselves to be pulled into the circle.

"I didn't know you ever danced," Lacey said. Would she always be finding out new things about them, she wondered?

The dance was a waltz, a mixer. For every sequence of the dance, there would be a new partner. As she instructed Grandpop and they began to dance, she realized that she had begun to be graceful. The music and Grandpop made it easy. One-two-three, one-two-three. As they changed partners, she spotted Grandmom and saw something light, even girlish, on Grandmom's face. Quickly, she looked back at Grandpop, who was beginning to smile as though he'd just caught a fine fish.

As if it had been planned, Grandmom wound up as Grandpop's partner for the last sequence, after which Ms. Lamb said, "Waltz your partner around the floor." Lacey couldn't dance for watching. Grandmom and Grandpop had found separate delight in dancing and now that they faced each other, they couldn't turn it off. Grandmom and Grandpop waltzed They knew how! They kept grinning at each other. This, Lacey thought, is part of my roots. Here was something else she hadn't known, these waltzing, smiling-at-each-other grandparents.

In the next day's mail came a check for two thousand dollars for the basket-weave-design saddle they'd sent to Colorado. Campbell held it and stared while Lacey shouted and leaped around. They caught up on the land payments and the taxes on the property and rented a truck to take the sections of railing to Asheville. Lacey couldn't keep her fingers off the iron starfire in her pocket.

"I'm so relieved to have it here," the man at the resort said, and he showed them the layout of a brochure about the resort. "There will be a picture of the railing here," he said. And beneath the spot where the picture would go were the words *Mountain-design railing by David Habib and Campbell Bittner.*

"Wow," Lacey said. It didn't matter one smidgen that her name was not there. Her name *was* there, for she was a part of Campbell and David, just like she was a part of Grandpop and Grandmom, and Kenny and Tam, just like this starfire in her pocket was a part of her and David and Campbell. They supervised the installation of the railing. No one but her and Campbell would ever know there was one trillium, one fire pink, and one David missing.

Back home, yellow violets popped up by the creek and, tinged with green, the dogwood blossoms opened, and the trillium was in bloom.

"Look, Campbell. Trillium. We've been here a year." They gazed out the trillium window, knowing how pleased David would be that they could see trillium twice, in the glass and beyond it.

Lacey stopped riding Polly and led her to the pasture to exercise at will. "Can I sleep in the barn so I can be there when my Starfire is born?" she asked.

"I don't see why not," Campbell said. "I know I won't have to worry about you freezing."

So she stayed in the barn at night and got up red-eyed from lack of sleep because she kept jumping up at every sound from the stall and it was only Polly, Polly alone. Still, there was school to go to and Campbell would not let her stay home. Even Tam asked every day, "Has the foal been born yet?" Maybe Tam didn't want to ride "no old horse," but she would love the young one, Lacey knew.

Then here came Campbell, to take her out of school. "It's happening," Campbell said. Time seemed to crawl as they inched from Savory to the barn. At the barn, they leaped out of the truck, leaving both doors open like wings.

They were too late for the birthing. Already standing on wobbly legs was a red filly with—like a miracle—a sort of star-shaped blaze on its forehead. Lacey needed fourteen hands for all the loving she wanted to give.

"Polly, Polly, oh, oh," she said, patting Polly, stooping to the foal. Her Starfire! Red as Polly. "Could anything be more perfect?" she said to Campbell, to Polly, to herself. Polly nibbled at her hair in pleasure. She cuddled the filly's head, stroked shoulders, sides, flanks, and legs, and touched the coarse hair of the short, flicking tail.

"Look, would you look?" she said, as though Campbell was not looking. She touched the blaze, outlining it with a fingertip, and in that moment she knew this filly was not her Starfire. "Look, Campbell, look," she said again. "What does this look like?"

"A star, baby. You have your Starfire."

"No, Campbell, look," Lacey said, still tracing. "It's a trillium. See? This is David's filly and her name is Trillium."

In celebration, Campbell announced Sunday dinner at the cabin, so everyone could come and see the foal.

"Campbell, let's just have dinner here," Kenny said. "Ever who wants can come see the foal before or after.

There's no need to upset Mama just when everything has finally smoothed out."

"We want it at our place," Lacey said. What was Kenny worried about? Did he think Grandmom wouldn't let things stay smoothed over? And what if she didn't? The rest of them would stay smoothed over, Lacey thought. She was surprised at who spoke up next.

"Ever who wants Sunday dinner with the family," said Marlene, "will have to come to Campbell's cabin."

Grandmom came. They all traipsed up to the barn to see Pretty Polly and Trillium. The "ooohs" and "ahhhs" and baby-talk kept Lacey grinning. Even Kenny talked gooshy. As the people moved back toward the cabin, Lacey led Polly across the paddock and into the pasture, and Trillium shimmied and pranced at her mother's side.

At the cabin, Grandmom held an enormous package behind her, as though it could be hidden. "I have a surprise," she said.

Lacey couldn't stop grinning. Grandmom had already surprised them, just by coming. We've melted them, David, she thought. It took a year and a death and a foal, but we melted them.

"I've finished the Bittner quilt," Grandmom said, rattling paper as she unwrapped it and opened it for all to see, "and I want to give it to Campbell and Lacey."

Lacey took a quick breath and looked at Campbell.

"Here's Thomas Elihu coming over the mountain," Grandmom said, showing the bearded man on an enormous horse. Had he had a beard when she'd seen this square before, Lacey wondered? Did Kenny think Thomas Elihu Bittner was a wimp?

"Here's Marlene with her nurse's cap, and Kenny under a car. There's Tam at flag corps, and Tina at the piano, and Teresa with a school book and a tooth out." Everyone peered forward as Grandmom slid the squares through her fingers. "Here's Tom." Everyone laughed, for she had him with a gas pump in one hand and a fishing rod in the other. "And Lacey." The flag, the fire pink, and the horse's head were expertly appliquéd.

"And Campbell."

Of course, there was Campbell. Even Grandmom wouldn't have made this quilt and given it to Campbell if she'd left Campbell off. There was a belt, a billfold, and a saddle. Lacey smiled and bit her lip. No symbols of Campbell's past life, symbols of Ann, but things that represented this current Ann Campbell Bittner, and Grandmom had even said "Campbell."

Campbell said "Mama," rather softly.

Then Grandmom said, "And here's David." The silence was louder than any thunder. The square depicted a strong hand wielding a hammer over an anvil and flames from a forge fire licked up behind.

The one who snuffled was Kenny. Then, with loud bluster, he said, "Let's all for godsakes eat."